CHRISTMAS MELODY

A Sweet Christmas Volume 8

SAMANTHA JACOBEY

Lavish
Publishing LLC

First Edition

A Sweet Christmas Series Book 8

2022 Lavish Publishing, LLC

All Rights Reserved

Published in the United States by Lavish Publishing, LLC, Midland, TX

Cover Design by: Victor R. Sosa

Cover Images: CanStock

Paperback Edition

ISBN: 978-1-64900-056-9

www.LavishPublishing.com

Contents

Prologue

DONNING HER FAVORITE JOGGING SHORTS, Candy quietly slipped from her bedroom, shoes in hand. Downstairs in the kitchen, she paused long enough to shove a sock-covered foot in each while leaning against the counter. She then started a pot of coffee, her ears listening for sounds in their giant, sleeping house; especially in the adjacent room occupied by her mother. Hearing nothing, she smiled at the soft orange light that indicated the brew had commenced. With one last glance around, she exited through the back door without a sound.

A few minutes later, she ran with loud clomps as her feet hit the sidewalk in the pre-dawn silence. Ahead of her, the light of Ben's porch glowed warmly. Slowing her pace, she smiled and waved. "I guess you made it," she teased as he fell into step beside her.

"I had to," he replied jovially. "I'm still working on my COVID twenty."

"You didn't gain twenty pounds," she rebuked, calling him out. "With all that lawn and gardening you did, you couldn't have."

"No, it wasn't twenty, but it was enough. Besides, I wanted

to have a few minutes of calm before the big day." He coughed a laugh at the joke. "All that estrogen. I'm surprised I survived living with them as long as I did."

Making the corner in stride, Candice hummed her agreement, "A big day indeed after all these months of waiting. Grace's adoption has gone smoothly, though. And you know the girls appreciate all your help with the legal stuff."

"I'll be glad when it's over," Benjamin lamented. Eyes straight ahead, his voice held a sour note.

Catching the subtle change, she glanced up at his masculine features outlined by the dim light of sunrise. "You ok?" she dared quietly.

His lips pursed, he hesitated to consider the query. "I really can't talk about it," he stated curtly.

Her arms pumping as she jogged easily beside him, Candy bit her bottom lip. *Of course he wants to talk about it*, she silently mused, suspecting it was the real reason he had joined her. As she waited calmly, he did not disappoint.

"I'm jealous as hell, that's all," he fumed a few yards later. His pace quickened and Candy increased her effort to remain beside him. "I love you guys," he gushed between heavy breaths. "The bubble has totally changed my life. My perspective. It has also made it incredibly hard. You know?" Glancing down at her, he could see the heightened color in her cheeks. "Jesus, Candy!" He dropped to a brisk walk.

"I'm fine," she gasped, secretly glad that he had. Placing a couple of fingers against her neck to feel her pulse beating wildly, she turned her wrist so she could see her stats on her monitoring device.

He stopped, doubling over and panting. "Melody and I've been talking again," he confessed quietly.

Using the short fence next to them, she stretched each leg in turn, silently waiting. Watching her, Ben grunted, "You don't have anything to say about that? No womanly advice to help a guy out?"

"Nope," she clipped, her hazel eyes flicking over at him. He glared at her, and she shrugged. "Melody is a friend, but I've seen how she hurts you. I don't think she means to, but she does. I thought you two were over for good," she finished with a frown. Glancing again at her arm band, she sighed. "I'll have to get back soon. The girls aren't coming today because of the adoption." She indicated the way they had come. "Mind if we walk?"

"Not at all." He chuckled quietly. "I ran you pretty hard," he confessed, then swallowed. "I guess I'm more upset than I want to admit."

Breathing easier at the slower pace, Candy inhaled deeply for a cleansing breath. "Ok, I'll give you my advice. But you aren't going to like it," she pointed out. Her hands gripped before her, she gushed, "I don't think Melody is a good match for you. I'm not sure she's a good match for anyone. I think if you keep holding on to whatever hope you're clinging to, you'll never have that family you've been wanting these last few years."

Rocking his jaw, Ben smoothed his damp locks with an open palm. "That's rather blunt, Candy."

"Sorry." She swung her hands anxiously, catching them in front of her once more to interlock her fingers. "You're my friend, too, Ben. I've played the matchmaker on you a few times. I thought you and Carol might make it, but that didn't work. I thought you and Holly might give it a go –"

He laughed loudly, cutting her off. "And you got me and Melody together."

"That wasn't really my fault," she jeered, recalling his taking her to an ordinary prenatal visit where the couple had met. "But yeah, I did think you would make a nice couple. You seemed so suited for each other. And everyone needs someone," she finished with a shrug.

Ben considered her final words in silence until they arrived back in front of the small cottage he called home. Only three doors down from the Ford's stately structure and the massive dwelling the girls occupied across the street from it, he had snatched it up the first day it had been on the market. Catching her shoulder, he smiled. "Don't let my troubles bother you. Especially today. I'll see you at the celebration on Saturday, if not before then."

Candy patted the hand, then took to a light jog as she finished the return home, ready to face the day.

ONE

One for the Team

Sitting in a small café across from the school, Candy tapped the laminate-covered table with her freshly painted nails. Her laptop open before her, she poured over the registration forms for the umpteenth time. With a final meeting scheduled with her degree advisor, she would register for her fall classes that afternoon. However, she had one more person she needed to talk to before she made any commitments.

Hearing the small bell on the door, she flicked her eyes over nervously, her heart skipping a beat when she recognized the older woman in her plain linen suit. "Glenda," she breathed, catching the word and using it to check her breath. Smiling at the minty fragrance, she hoped she appeared relaxed as their adoption advocate approached her booth next to the front glass.

"Candice Ford," Glenda Tucker greeted more cheerfully than usual. "How nice to see you! How's our girl?"

Candy giggled, recalling how miserable their visits had been four years prior. "Our ebony angel is a true miracle," she replied airily, indicating for her to sit. "Thank you again for all that you did to bring her into our family."

"All I did was ensure our procedures were given their due

diligence." Glenda adjusted herself onto the vinyl-covered bench. Shoving her purse into the empty space between her and the short wall, she glanced out the window. "Have you finished?" she asked, indicating the university across the way.

"Uh, no," Candy stammered. Swallowing, she closed her computer slowly, having hoped the small talk would last a little longer. "Actually, that's why I wanted to meet with you. It's the final day of registration, and I can't wait any longer," she confessed almost in a whisper.

"Candy, what's wrong?" Glenda's sharp blue eyes studied her downturned features. "You appear almost in a panic."

"Do I?" Reaching for her sweat-covered glass, Candy's hand shook. Deciding against trying to lift it, she withdrew the appendage and wiped the digits on her pant leg under the table. "I need your advice," she dared. "I told my family last Christmas that I had made my final decision on my degree. But I want to be sure." She stared into the crystal blue orbs glaring at her. "I need to know if I have what it takes," she stated flatly.

"For what?" Glenda asked crisply, her stern features set in their familiar rigidness.

"To do what you do," Candy breathed. "I want to be a counselor. I want to help others, like you, but I'm scared –" her voice cracked, ending in an emotional sob. "What if I've put in all these hours and work, but I'm not good enough to help... girls like me."

Glenda's smile spread slowly. "Oh, Candy," she whispered. "For all your strength, you still harbor such fear."

"Yes," Candy snorted, reaching for napkins from the holder between them. Tearing a few free, she used them to stem her flow of tears. "God, I'm such a mess!" Wiping her red-tipped nose, she scowled. "I practiced being calm and cool all morning, and then as soon as you show up, I freak." Applying the coarse paper to her eyes, she dabbed angrily at her hot tears.

Panic had indeed risen within her, and her inability to control it, or hide it, tore her apart.

"Why do you want to do this?" Glenda asked, crossing her legs to fold her hands on top of them, seemingly unmoved by the display.

"Because I don't want to see girls suffer the way that I have," Candy answered stiffly, her resolve broken. All she could do now was get through this and make it to her meeting. "I'm sorry I bothered you. I'm sure you're busy."

"I still eat lunch," Glenda clipped, her chin rising as the waitress approached. "I need a ham on rye with potato salad," she ordered coolly.

"And your drink?" the server prodded.

"An unsweet tea." Glenda glanced at her companion across from her.

Clicking a few selections on her tablet, the girl continued, "What about you? You want a refill?"

Candy shook her head, her honey-colored locks framing her flushed cheeks. "I'll have the baked potato though, thanks. Make it loaded."

"Coming right up." The slender server pivoted to leave them.

Watching her go, Candy's shoulders slumped. "You know about Bella and Grace," she pointed out evenly.

"Yes, I'm aware of the private adoption of her child by your friends. Did you have a hand in that?" She accepted her beverage and waited for Candy to decide on her reply.

"Not exactly." Candy watched the waitress as she moved between the tables. "I mean, Bella came to me, and I did my best to help her. But in the end, she's the one who chose the girls to adopt her baby. And they didn't need any persuading to take her." She smiled at the thought of how last Christmas had played out. "It was all so tangled. Complicated."

"And you don't see your influence on the end result," Glenda concluded.

Candy's hazel orbs snapped back to the woman across from her. "I worked very hard to ensure whatever happened was Bella's choice," she hissed. "I didn't let anyone pressure her. Not even Billy."

"You protected her," Glenda quipped, stifling a grin as she stirred sweetener into her drink.

"You're damn right I did," Candy snapped, anger boiling just below the surface.

"I think you have what it takes." The social worker smiled openly. "You'll have to perfect your presentation. You can't afford to get caught up in emotional displays, but that will come in time."

Candy gaped at her. "And you know this, how?"

"Because of your spirit." Candy's hand resting on the table, Glenda used her own to cover it. Giving it a squeeze, she reassured, "You have to be strong to do what I do, and you are."

"But I'm afraid of everything," Candy lamented, not withdrawing from the stranger's familiar touch.

"Do you face those fears?"

Candy blinked at her.

"You seem to have survived." Lifting the hand, Glenda used it to indicate the woman across from her. "You have and care for a special needs son and a daughter of a different race, successfully from what I've seen. Plus, you have another child, who was born during a pandemic, no less."

"I have help with them," Candy pointed out glibly, making room for their plates to be placed before them.

"And you believe that having the involvement of others negates your efforts," Glenda teased. "You think the members of a winning soccer team can't claim their victories because they didn't do it alone."

Candy laughed, using a fork to chop at her spud vigorously. "No, of course not! They're a team. I'm not."

"We are all a team, Candice. None of us do it all alone, no matter how badly we might like too." She indicated their meal. "The waitress only brought it to us. She couldn't do that without the cook."

"What are you saying?" Candy snapped, still perturbed at the seeming nonsense.

"I'm saying, you're ready and able to do what I do. If that's what you want, and it appears that it is. All you have to do is accept that it will never be entirely up to you." Glenda took a few bites, letting her think on that before she added, "There will always be ups and downs. Wins and losses. Finish your degree, and then find yourself the right team. Together, you can be that person you want to be. At least most of the time."

Digging into her gooey potato, Candy ate in silence, her mind turning the advice. Her emotions rising and falling across her features, Glenda watched the process with interest. When her sandwich and side were gone, she finished her drink and reached for her bag.

"I need to get back to the office. It was good to see you," she stated firmly. "Let me know when you graduate, and I'll see what I can do as far as helping you locate a position."

"A job?" Candy looked up at her in surprise. "You'd give me a recommendation? You hardly know me."

"I know you better than you think." Glenda chuckled. "It comes with the territory," she assured, giving Candy's shoulder a squeeze before she turned away. Her heels clicked against the floor as she crossed to the register and closed out her check. With hardly a glance in the girl's direction, she pushed on the glass door, causing the bell to jingle as she stepped into the warm afternoon sun.

TWO

An Annual Affair

BEN SAT CROOKED in the seat of his Mercedes. With his left elbow propped against the window, his fingers toyed with his smooth lips. His right hand gripped the steering wheel, anxiously giving it a squeeze as his car crept forward on the narrow lane. From his peripherals, people bustled along the sides of the street as the sun sank low on the horizon. "Halloween," he muttered, glancing at the clock to note the time.

Pulling up in front of a well-kept townhome, he killed the engine. Glaring at the front door through the passenger side glass, he resisted the urge to honk at his date. Impatiently tapping his thumb against the leather grip, he thought about the party they would soon join across town. Again, he looked at the luminated device, waiting for the last minute to tick by.

When the number flicked from twenty-nine to thirty, he briskly opened the car door and stepped out into the cool air. Laughter echoed in the distance, curling his lips for a moment. Rounding the front of the vehicle, his dress shoes clicked against the concrete walk. He had hardly worn his best suit since the pandemic started, but knowing who would attend the Fords' annual gathering, he had dressed for the occasion.

Climbing the single step to the portal, he gave the hard wood a firm rap, then withdrew the hand quickly when it opened immediately.

Benjamin grinned at her, but the emotion faded when Melody hissed, "I'm not going."

"What?" he croaked. Through the six-inch crack, he could see her fluffy mauve housecoat pulled tightly across her chest. He had come to pick her up this time, and by appearances, his instincts had been right; if he had let her drive herself, she would have simply stood him up. Placing a hand on the flat surface, he gave it a shove. "I'm not going without you!"

His voice loud, the push caught her off guard. Her eyes widened and the cry that escaped her trembling lips held him from crossing the threshold. "Why not?" he demanded harshly. "You can't keep doing this to me, Mel."

"It's not about you," she muttered. Her left hand holding the door in place, her right traced the edges of her robe and pulled them tighter at her neck. "I'm sick," she stated flatly. "I've got chicken noodle on the stove."

"Fine, let me cancel our appearance, and I'll settle for a bowl of soup." He stared at her, waiting for her to step back and let him in, or to close the door in his face. When she did neither, he pulled his phone from his pocket and turned around. Stepping off the stoop and onto the walk as the phone rang, he heard the door click shut behind him.

"Candy, hi!" he called louder than necessary.

"Hey, Ben!" The petite blonde giggled on the other end. "You're missing dinner," she teased.

"Yeah, I know." He blew a disgusted breath out through his nostrils. "Melody isn't feeling well, so we're going to have something light at her place. I'm sorry we won't be able to make it."

Inside the house, Melody leaned her forehead against the door frame and listened to him make his apologies on the other side. His tone lower, she could hear the disappointment in his muffled words. She gripped the handle tightly while she breathed in deep and slow. Exhaling, she closed her eyes and waited, considering twisting the lock and leaving him there.

"Yeah, I know. Maybe we can try again at Christmas," Ben negotiated. "Anyway, tell the kids to have fun and be safe!" He dropped the device and ended the call so he didn't have to listen to the festivities in the background any longer. Sucking his lips in, he bit them gently.

Before this night, he had only stood at that door twice, and each time she had come out and climbed into his car without giving him so much as a peek inside. He stared at the smooth, black finish of his ride that lost its sharpness as the light faded. "Melody!" he called, pivoting to return to his knocking, but as he made the step, she flung the portal open and glared at him.

"Stop." She held up a hand, indicating her intention. "I said I don't feel well. Go home, and maybe I'll be on to Skype after I rest."

"I don't want to Skype," he groaned, reaching the threshold with the tips of his polished toes. "I want to come in. Mel, it's been months and months. We can't go on forever –" he stopped abruptly. He had seen the fear in her eyes when he pushed on the door, but only sadness remained. "Baby, talk to me. Please." Candy had warned him weeks ago that Melody would only ever hurt him, and in that instant, he wished that he had listened.

Her bottom lip dimpled as she gathered her resolve. "I don't let people in here," she bit through a tight jaw.

"What's that supposed to mean?" he stammered. "Like, since the pandemic?" His features twisted as confusion filtered across them.

"No. Since ever." A tear spilled over, and she swiped it away. Frustrated, she stamped a foot as she shook her bright red locks. "You aren't going to give up, are you."

"No," he replied firmly. Inside, he could smell actual cooking. "Is that really chicken soup?"

"Pot pie," she confessed. "I had it delivered from Ruby's." Her chin lowered, she cut her guilty gaze up at him. "I'm sorry, Ben," she breathed.

"Don't be sorry. Just let me in," he pleaded gently. "Whatever it is, we can face it together. Besides." He shrugged, folding his arms across his chest. "I love Ruby's."

"Was that Ben?" Gary asked as Candy rejoined the table.

"Unfortunately, yes," she replied glumly. "They aren't coming."

Her fork poised in midair, Eve pointed out tartly, "That woman isn't good for him."

"Well, we don't get to decide that," Candy mumbled, thinking of Glenda. "And we have happier things to talk about," she pushed. She smiled at the Doubletrees, who sat across from her. The family gathering larger than ever, their immediate family sat around the dining room table, while a second group ate in the kitchen with the children, which included Holly, Carol, Billy and Bell. "I take it Bella is having a good year?"

"Yes," Annette agreed, nodding her approval. "She is back on track with her grades at least."

"I think having Grace changed her," Matthew pointed out with a shake of his head. "She is far more focused than she has ever been."

"That's good news," Candy confirmed, forcing a large smile. "I heard Billy say he was enjoying the JC, and I'll be graduating before we know it. It's wonderful, really."

Next to her, Gary only grunted as he glared at the two empty chairs.

THREE

Wilderness

MELODY'S GAZE THOUGHTFUL, her eyes skimmed up and down Benjamin's tall, masculine frame. "You look nice."

"I dressed for the occasion," he replied calmly. "An evening with good friends and my best girl."

She grinned, her green orbs jumping to meet his. "I guess I can't keep you outside forever." She stepped back, permitting him to enter, but as he brushed past, she moved to keep the gap between them beyond arm's length. "Close the door," she instructed.

Giving it a push, Ben turned the deadbolt as well, then followed her form as it floated down the entry hall, which opened into a large living area. Beyond that lay the source of the delicious aroma.

Leaving him in the sitting area, Mel crossed the section of carpet that held a small dinette. "You can sit here," she proposed, indicating one of the wooden chairs.

Watching her, Benjamin's heart thumped loudly within his chest. Clearly a woman's house, he compared it to the stark contrast of his own. Comfy twin chairs and a sofa adorned with a half-dozen or so pillows created an arc that faced a plain television in the left-hand corner. His fingers trailed the table that ran the back of the couch, noting the few figurines that adorned it.

To the right of the grouping, a small fireplace separated them and the table. Indicating the stone alcove's immaculate appearance, he asked, "You don't use this?" He placed his dinner jacket over the stiff back and took a seat in the chair closest to the wall a few feet from it.

"It's fake," she admitted, then shrugged. "Well, not fake really. It has gas, so I don't have to clean it."

"Hmm," he moaned, smiling at her. "You're a pretty self-sufficient lady."

At the far end of the dinette, she placed a plate of chicken pie on the flat surface and slid it towards him. Cautiously, he extended a long arm to catch the edge and drag it the rest of the way, then accepted a glass of wine offered in the same manner. Watching her fix her own, he pondered her actions and the oddity of her serving technique. "You really don't have guests often."

Melody ignored the remark and took a seat on the far end, her plate before her. The six feet of wood between them, she adjusted her robe and peered anxiously around her.

Using his fork, Ben picked at the flaky crust. "Ruby's is the best," he stated before having a small bite.

"Yes. I have it often." Her fingers still clutching the top of her robe, she watched him.

"I didn't realize I made you so nervous," he pointed out when she didn't join in the consumption.

Melody swallowed. "I have something to tell you."

"I bet." He grinned at her, lifting his glass as he relaxed against the back of the chair. "I'm all ears."

Her voice soft, only the silence of the house allowed her to be heard. "Like I said, I don't have company."

I don't let people in here, Ben recalled her exact words, and he briefly pondered if she actually meant the house. Aloud, he cajoled, "You have a beautiful home. It's a shame not to share it," and continued to casually pick at his plate.

Her tongue flicking over her lips, her voice quavered. "Ben, I'm androphobic."

He paused mid bite. "You're afraid of people?"

"Men, specifically." She blinked at him rapidly with a furrowed brow.

Lowering his fork, he gaped at her. "That's rather irrational," he muttered.

"Precisely," she clipped. "That's why it's called a phobia." She sniffed loudly, the chair creaking as she shifted on the cushioned seat. "I've battled with it most of my life, but the last few years..." her voice trailed away.

"We've been in a pandemic the last few years," he pointed out bluntly, confusion clouding his thoughts.

"Yes. Being locked away from others so many months has only heightened my response." Reaching for her glass, she gulped at the liquid, sloshing it inside the crystal.

Catching the motion, Ben's heart plummeted. "Baby, you're terrified." A tear spilled onto her cheek as she avoided his gaze. "Melody, I would never hurt you. Why didn't you tell me about this?" All the months they had chatted over the distance and devices, she had never said a word.

"This isn't something I share with anyone," she grunted. "Other than my therapist."

"And its men. I mean, only men," he clarified.

"Yes." Her eyes misty when they finally met his, she sighed. "I've learned how to avoid, or at least limit, male contact. I even chose a career that means I work exclusively with women."

A million questions flooded his brain, but tightening his jaw a few times, he pushed them back. There would be time for them at some point, if he were careful. For now, she had let him in, and he would allow her to expose her secrets when she was ready. "I see."

Silence seemed to crowd in around them, as if the weight of his tacit curiosity filled the room. With a clumsy grasp, Melody lifted her fork and busied herself with her dinner.

Taking slow bites as well, Ben remained as still as he could, his movements slow and purposed. She appeared to calm, her posture relaxing as the minutes ticked by. When the plates had been cleaned, he gently pushed his towards the center of the table. Folding his arms before him, he leaned against them.

"Thank you," he murmured. "Dinner was delicious."

"I'm sorry I didn't tell you. It wasn't right of me to hide my condition. I just thought –" she inhaled sharply, ending abruptly.

"It's ok," he soothed. "I understand, and more than you know. But you did mention a therapist. Does that mean you're planning to one day…" He paused, searching for the right words. "I don't want to sound insensitive," he confessed.

"One day be normal?" she provided for him.

"Yes." He nodded. "I don't think you plan on hiding in this little condo forever."

"No, someday I think I'll be ready," she agreed. Standing, she gathered the dishes, the table still between them. Always between them.

Firmly planted on the cushion, Ben never moved more than his arms, giving no indication of invading her world further. He felt as if he had entered a sacred forest and needed to be still to let the wilderness of animals there become accustomed to his presence. "I won't push you," he stated gruffly. "Take your time."

"Would you like dessert?" she asked, her tone still low, but her movements more fluid.

"I'd love some." He smiled, eying the box he felt certain held one of Ruby's famous cakes. Maintaining the grin, he watched her every move as she cut and plated, and then presented the decedent layers. "Can I get more wine?" He held up the empty goblet, then placed it on the table and slid it towards her.

Reaching to accept it, Melody straightened slowly. Biting her bottom lip, she sighed. "This all seems rather silly, doesn't it."

"No." His tone low, matching hers, he shook his head. "I'm happy you have let me in. But I do have a request."

Retrieving the bottle, she filled both glasses and sat it on the table. Pushing his beverage towards him, she prodded, "And that is?"

"I want you to let me help you. Let us help you."

"Us?" her eyes wide, her breath quickened. "Surely you don't mean…"

"Exactly. I have a group of close friends who adore me. And you. Candy and the other girls are your friends, too, Mel."

"Yes, I know that, but I can't tell them about this!" She sank into her seat in defeat. "Do you have any idea how embarrassing it would be for them to know?"

"Do you have any idea how lonely your life will be if you don't?"

She glowered at him. "Yes, I am aware of how lonely my life is," she groused. "The time I have spent on zoom and Skype with you have been more fulfilling than I ever imagined."

"So come with me then. Take the next step," he offered gently.

"Please don't tell them about this," she begged.

"No. I'm not going to tell them," he assured. "You are."

Her eyes wide, she inhaled in shallow pants. "My therapist has spoken of this for years. How I should reach out to someone I trust."

"You trust me, don't you, love?" He raised his glass, as if to toast her. "I promise, I won't let you fall."

"You can't promise me that," she challenged. "You don't know what it's like when the panic consumes you." She swiped at tears that trickled onto her flushed cheeks.

"Ok, I'll be there then, to catch you when you do." He wanted so badly to reach for her. To feel her flesh and squeeze her hand with his sturdy grasp. "I've got you, Melody," he whispered instead.

FOUR

Not His Circus

HIS SHOES SCUFFING against the sidewalk as he strutted down the walk, Ben slowly turned the events of the evening before. Shocked by Melody's confession, his disbelief had quickly fallen into dedicated reassurance. He had heard many times that long distance relationships were hard, but he had fallen for the redhead in the midst of one. He wanted desperately to grow that connection; to nurture the bud into a full bloom of love and devotion that would last them both a lifetime. Only now he realized the true width of the chasm between them, and he would do anything to help Melody cross it.

Arriving at the Ford homestead, he glanced across the street. "I need to give that yard one last mow," he muttered fondly, briefly thinking of the girls and the room he had once occupied in their manor.

Turning to the right, he sauntered up the drive and into the back yard, where he found Gary raking leaves. Around him, two small figures were doing their best to negate his efforts. "Looks like you have your hands full," he called as he approached.

"Yeah, these guys are having a ball." Gary laughed, pausing

his tool to watch Joycean and Lane, their peals of laughter filling the autumn air. "We missed you last night," he added somberly as the other man reached him.

"I know." Ben shrugged, offering open palms. "But Melody and I really needed to talk."

Gerald leaned against his handle and eyed him warily, afraid of what that conversation might have entailed. However, his friend's relationship was not his circus, nor had he been invited to comment upon it.

Hearing the silence, Benjamin shoved his hands into his pockets and grinned sheepishly. "I promised not to divulge, but I assure you that Melody will be stopping by. You will all get to hear her news then."

"Her news?" Gary's lips puckered, almost relieved it had not been "their news" they should anticipate.

"Is Candy home?" Ben ignored Gary's inquiry. "I've got a favor to ask of her and the girls." He rocked anxiously between his heels and toes, then sighed. "And of you."

"Ut-oh," Gary grunted, scowling as he turned his back and returned to his work.

Watching his friend's angry movements, Ben hesitated. He had promised not to give away Melody's secret but found it difficult to say what he needed to say without doing so. "Look, Gary. I know you and I have become friends."

"Like family," Gary corrected, still dragging his rake across the dying grass.

"Like family," Ben agreed, his voice losing its luster. "Gary, I need you to stay away from her."

Gary's head popped up as he swung to face the other man squarely. "What?"

"Melody has issues with men." His silver-streaked hair glinting in the morning sun, he couldn't have made the statement more confusing if he had tried. "I need you to give her a lot of space, at least until she is ready to share with you."

Gary's nose crinkled and his eyes narrowed. "Are you saying Melody has a problem with me?" He had only met the woman a few times, and at a distinct distance at that. In fact, he wasn't sure they had ever spoken directly.

"With men." Ben nodded slowly. "All men." Seeing the understanding register slowly as Gary's features softened before him, Benjamin smiled sheepishly. "I promised her I wouldn't tell, so please don't say anything to Candy. Let Melody share this. I think she needs to take that first step on her own."

"Well, you should at least warn the girls this is coming." Gary pulled at one of his gloves, ready to give up on his chore. "Is that really a thing?" he asked in bewilderment.

"Apparently it is, and it explains a lot." Ben relaxed at his friend's less aggressive stance. "I know things haven't been easy for her. I once found solace in our bubble, and I'm hoping she will as well."

Removing the other covering, Gary causally leaned the rake against the porch rail. Raising his hand, he indicated his youngest children. "We'll stay out here a bit longer and give you some time to talk with the girls. They're all in there." He raised a stiff thumb, vaguely indicating the back of the house, and added, "Doing what women do."

Ben grinned at the other man knowingly. Together, they and Roger had lived in a sea of estrogen for months, with women on all sides. They had survived largely by relying on each other, and he suddenly felt glad he had confided in one of his closest friends, knowing the other man would never let him down.

FIVE

Uncle Ben

BEN LET himself in through the back door, closing it gently behind him. "Hello?" he called, his eyes skimming the perimeter of the empty, well-kept kitchen.

"In the living room," a female voice beckoned through the connecting arch.

Arriving at the threshold, Benjamin grinned broadly. Carol and Holly each held an end of the sofa, while Lanelle sat in her favorite chair. Nestled in the older woman's arms, baby Grace ate eagerly at her bottle. "Aww," he moaned. "Where's Candy?"

Holly extended a digit, not looking up from her book. "In the office. She's got a tight schedule this fall."

"Tight," her lover grunted. "That girl signed up for a full load and then some this semester."

"She did?" Ben gasped, angling for an empty chair and taking a seat.

"I think she's tired of school," Holly defended, closing her reading material and placing it on the table beside her. "She can see the end and is in a hurry to get there."

"Well, I hate to disturb her." Ben stared at the passage, hesitation in his voice. Turning to the group, he scooted to the edge for a better view of the pudgy-faced infant. "I guess I could talk to you girls, and you can tell Candy later."

"Tell me what?" Candice asked as she entered in time to hear her name. Ben laughed, his flushed face giving her a giggle. "That juicy, huh? I needed a break anyway. Let me make coffee, and then you can tell."

"I'll get the coffee," Caroline offered, vacating Candy's favorite spot on the couch.

From his seat on the fringe of the cushion, Ben watched his former housemate slip into the kitchen. Listening to the clatter of caffeine preparations, he wrung his hands anxiously. "Can you hear me in there?" he called through the wall.

"I hear you fine," came a crisp reply.

"Good," he shouted back, "because I only want to explain this once."

"Just spit it out, dear," Lanelle advised, still cuddling her prize.

"Yeah," he coughed. "But I have to be careful what I say. I promised Melody that I would let her tell you." He pondered Gary's advice, his head hanging for a moment. "But I think I should warn you."

Frowning, Candy grew uncomfortable in her relaxed position. Scooting to the front half of her seat, she leaned forward. "Ben, has something happened to Melody?"

"Uh, no. Not exactly." Deciding to take his friend's advice, he shrugged. "Mel has a condition. All of the times she has stood me up. Or us up." He glanced around the group to see all eyes were on him, and he sat up to make room for a tray of mugs to be placed on the ottoman and served. "Melody needs our help, guys. As badly as she wanted to join us, she hasn't been able to overcome her fear."

Holly stiffened. "Is this something you should be telling us? If this is a medical condition, it really isn't your place."

"I know that," Ben assured, selecting a cup. "And I'm not going to tell you what it is. But I want you to be ready, because I'm going to get her over here. Finally get her here. And she can tell you, but I want you to be prepared."

Candy's breathing shallow, she studied him for a long moment, then selected her own serving of brew. Her voice trembling, she almost whispered, "Melody isn't sick, is she?"

"It's not that kind of condition." Ben took a noisy sip and tried again. "It's more of a phobia or that type of disorder. It's made her a prisoner in her own life. I want to bring her out and let her start slow, hear in the bubble."

Taking the center cushion on the sofa, Carol stated airily, "But Melody is a doctor," as if that prevented the other woman from having such a thing.

"Well, apparently this has been a long-time struggle for her, and has greatly influenced the choices in her life," Ben pointed out gruffly. "I won't say any more. Just be ready to accept whatever she says with open minds."

"When is she coming?" Candy asked timidly. She had faced her own mental issues, and with her choice of careers firmly in focus, she could see the encounter as a test of her readiness for such a future.

"Soon. For dinner tonight if you girls don't mind having her. I'll take Gary and the kids out to dinner. Uncle Ben night or something, so it can be just the girls," he schemed.

"Oh, why don't we take her out instead?" Carol asked innocently. "A girls' night out could be fun!"

"No!" Ben almost shouted, then ran his hand through his hair to calm himself. "She would be better off here. This is a safe place. Not like a restaurant or bar. Anything like that."

"What kind of condition is this?" Candy asked, her eyes fixed on his tense features.

"That kind," he countered, meeting her gaze and giving her a firm nod.

Understanding fully, Holly intervened. "At home will be fine, then. We'll make a small dinner and give her plenty of room. But you, Gary and the kids can have your meal here and we can gather at our place. We can cook the meal for you and leave it in the oven. That way, they can go to bed at regular time, even if the evening grows long."

"Yes," Carol agreed, thinking of Dakota as she glanced at Candy. "Would that be all right with you?"

"Fine, fine," Candice agreed, toying with her lip. Uncertain as to the root of the issue, she could say one thing for certain; the scenario would serve as a real-life test. She hoped all would go well, helping their friend and confirming her readiness that Glenda had so strongly attested to.

SIX

Hiding the Hurt

WALKING TO BEN'S CAR, Melody ran her hands anxiously over her fall-print dress. Although she adored the man, she had only followed through with outings with him twice, and both times she had contrived a picnic lunch to hold on her lap just to avoid taking his hand. He had never guessed the reason behind her insisting on dates at the park, nor at how much courage it had taken for her to make it through them.

But with her secret out, it would be pointless to pretend any longer. Slipping into the leather seat when he opened the passenger door, she held her breath as he closed it behind her. Her eyes fixed on his masculine frame as he rounded the front, she dug her nails into the palms of her hands and willed herself to be calm.

Sliding in behind the wheel, a large console between them, Ben kept to his side of the vehicle. "Are you good?" he asked as they pulled away from the curb.

Inhaling through her nose, she exhaled slowly before she whispered, "I'm going to be fine." She felt certain if she said it enough times, it might actually turn out to be true. The wide space between them empty, she grinned. "This car was practically made for us."

"Yes, it certainly made it easy to keep your distance," he agreed with a genuine grin.

She bristled at the verbal barb. "I'm sorry. I wish I could be more normal for you," she confessed.

He gripped the wheel tightly. "You are normal, baby. Don't sell yourself short."

"It's kind of you to say so." She turned her attention to the window and monitored her breathing, knowing better.

Arriving at the wide drive of Carol and Holly's house, Ben stopped and cut off the engine. Reversing the process, Melody stood on the edge of their grass a moment later. Looking up at the sliding glass door on their patio, she grimaced.

"Don't worry," he assured, purposely taking a step back as if they were social distancing. "The girls have a wonderful evening planned for you, and I'll be right across the street if you need me." He waved his phone at her and beamed. "Text nine-one-one to me and I'll be here in a flash."

Her lips curled into a surly grin, she nodded. Seeing Caroline's slender frame appear briefly through the glass, she cringed. "I guess I never realized what a big place this was."

"Ten bedrooms," Ben provided easily. "A small mansion, really."

"That's a lot of house for two women and a baby," Melody pointed out, unable to budge. "Do you think they would agree to eat outside?"

"Don't worry, it'll only be you and the girls. Candy is coming, but Lanelle and the rest of us are dining at their house." He indicated the other dwelling and Candice Ford crossing the asphalt. "Here she comes now."

"I see her," Melody agreed through a tight jaw. "Telling them will be harder than I thought."

"Don't worry. They've all faced struggles. They'll understand." Taking a few steps backwards, he pivoted to greet the shorter woman as they passed each other. "Kid gloves," he warned under his breath.

"No worries," Candy replied in kind. Her smile broad, she squealed, "Melody! It's amazing to finally have you here!"

How many times had she stood them up by now? The redhead couldn't begin to count. "Hi, Candy," she replied evenly, offering a side hug. When they were close, she mumbled, "I'm really nervous."

"Don't be." Candy gave her a firm squeeze. "It's the four of us and Grace, of course. A simple little girl get-together."

Melody dropped the embrace, wondering what Ben had said to them. "He told you, then," she accused.

"Only that you were afraid to come and that you needed friends," Candy assured. Grasping an elbow, she guided her doctor up the path and towards the door. Halfway up, she added, "The rest is up to you."

Her heart thumping, the taller woman nodded and presented bright features she didn't quite feel when they reached the entrance to go inside. Melody had learned to pretend and how to hide the hurt she always felt. She would give it her best to mask the turmoil inside her. "Ladies. So good to see you again. Do I get to hold the baby?"

"I need to change her, and then you can have her as long as you like," Holly agreed.

"I'll set the table," Candy volunteered, while searching the fridge for the wine.

At the stove, Caroline hummed to herself as she prepared the dishes to be presented. "We have two bottles of your favorite over in the back."

"I see them." Candice groaned as she leaned forward to fish them out.

Her eyes darting around her, Melody paused to take it all in. "Your décor is lovely. Did you renovate?"

"During the pandemic, yes." Holly held out a squirming infant. "She'll take a bottle now, if you want to feed her."

"There wasn't much else to do," Caroline dropped airily as she placed their salads on the table and offered Melody the feeding. "And Ben living here made it super easy. I never knew he could be so handy."

"Still, it's such a big place," Melody lamented, accepting the formula and choosing a seat. Curling the child into her arms, she recalled having delivered her earlier in the year. "I never really get to see them after they arrive."

"Well, when you come around more, you'll get to see this one all the time," Holly pointed out as she joined her in an adjacent chair.

"And Lane," Candy added as she poured glasses for them and took the other side, leaving Carol the seat opposite their guest.

Gracie's eyes closed as she suckled, but Melody held her long after the feeding had ended, and the sleeping commenced. Placing the empty container on the table, she used her freed hand to have a few bites of salad, noting the others had all but finished theirs. "I'm sorry. I'm holding up the meal."

"We're casual," Carol countered, swirling her glass. "And yes, the house is enormous. But now that it's finished, we do have plans for it."

"More adoptions?" Candy teased, her plate empty as well.

"Actually, having Bella here was inspiring," Holly clipped, leaning on her elbows and watching her daughter rest against Melody's bosom. "We've been discussing having a few other women or girls in need come for a stay. I'm leaning towards those over ordinary renters."

"Are you serious?" Candy gasped, her thoughts on Glenda

and their private conversation before registration. "That would be amazing!"

"It's not settled," Carol pointed out coolly. Standing, she gathered the plates and moved to serve the next course. "There's a great deal of planning that would need to be done if we were to open our rooms to strangers."

"Yes, but could you imagine the impact?" Candy beamed. "Wow. I had no idea you were even considering such a thing." Glancing at Melody, she flushed. "Oh, and we've neglected our guest. Mel, are you ready to tell us the news that Ben promised?"

Curling the babe to her chest a bit tighter, Melody hid behind the smaller body for a moment. A tear dripping onto her cheek, she swiped it away and shrugged, having hoped they had forgotten. She had known it would be difficult, but at the moment her throat seemed to clamp shut at the thought of speaking.

"Take your time. We have two more servings and dessert," Caroline informed them tartly from the stove.

"And more wine in the basement if we need it," Holly agreed.

"Thank you," Melody whispered, then blurted, "but I might as well. I have androphobia. It means I'm afraid of men."

The next round of dishes delivered, Carol sank onto her seat and gaped at her across the table between them. Her face scrunched, she struggled to reconcile the other woman's words. "How does that work? I thought Ben was your boyfriend. Aren't you guys sleeping together?"

A deep red hue tinted Melody's cheeks as she gasped. "Certainly not."

Exchanging a glance, Candy and Holly each understood the situation in an instant. Coming to her defense, Candice proclaimed, "Maybe we should let it sink in while we finish the meal. Then we can talk."

"Agree," Holly seconded. Using her fork, she indicated the immaculate plate. "Carol, darling, you have out done yourself."

"I found a few new recipes," her lover replied, her gaze still fixed on the redhead. "I'm sorry. I didn't mean to embarrass you," she hissed.

"Think nothing of it." Hoisting her glass, Melody gulped her beverage. Returning the near empty to the table, she picked at her serving as she smoldered.

The air stifling around them, Candy sighed. The elephant in the room looming larger than ever, she groaned, "I shouldn't have asked."

Cutting her green orbs over at her, Melody's lip quivered. Fortunately, Grace held down her arm and prevented her from texting Ben at that precise moment. "I think a half-way house to help mothers in need would be a splendid cause."

Candy grinned at her attempt at the safer subject. "Wouldn't it." She glared at Carol, hoping her housekeeper would agree to the simple subject, at least for the time being.

Refraining from pushing, Carol sulked as they completed the course, and then the next. When they came to the dessert, she declared, "Now can we talk about Ben?"

"About Ben?" Melody glared at her, failing to make the connection.

"Yes. What did he do that made you afraid of men?" Caroline snapped, angry at her previous employer and his assumed crime against their friend.

"Ben!" Melody giggled, the other two women briefly joining her. "He didn't do anything. I've had this problem off and on for years, hon."

Carol's turn to flush, a soft pink stained her cheeks. "Oh. So how does it work then?"

Across from her, Holly cleared her throat. "Well, obviously, she has some function." She turned her attention to the doctor and grinned. "You have a well-established practice."

"Yes. In a field with little to no interaction with males," Melody confessed. "Other than the occasional companion at delivery, I have near zero contact."

"And that's healthy?" Candy asked as she savored her rich chocolate cake. "This is delicious, by the way," she praised.

"I would never consider a phobia healthy." Melody chuckled. Shifting, she confessed, "My arm has gone to sleep. I hate to give her up, but it might be time to put her down."

"I'll take her," Carol offered.

While the slender blonde delivered her daughter to the nursery, the remaining trio moved to the family room to finish their cake and wine. "So you've lived with this struggle for a while," Holly observed as she claimed a cushioned chair.

"I was diagnosed in my early twenties," Melody explained, dropping her shoes on the floor and curling her feet beneath her in her own seat. "Although, I experienced odd feelings of panic for some time before that. High school was a mess, I assure you."

"You hide it well," Candy commended, considering the implications such a condition might have.

"I've had lots of practice. And I've structured my life to avoid triggers." Melody sipped from her glass thoughtfully. "If it weren't for Ben, I might have lived the rest of my life with this secret while hiding in the shadows."

"So, Benjamin does have something to do with it," Carol declared as she rejoined them.

"Only as a catalyst for change." Melody grinned at her friend. "He cares for me, and I want to overcome this fear inside me. I want to have dinner with him and not spend the entire time trembling in terror."

"You said he cares for you," Holly observed. "Does that mean you also care for him?"

"Of course I do!" Melody sat up straight on her cushion. "Oh, God! Is it not apparent?" Her eyes darted around the circle of women. "I love Ben. The pandemic was such a lonely time. My practice down to the bare bones, I seldom saw or spoke to anyone other than cases."

Candy nodded, recalling the precautions. "You didn't even have your receptionist or clerks in the office with you."

"No. I was truly alone." Melody's eyes grew misty. "I thought I would prefer it that way, but over time it became so empty. When Ben gave me his number, I laughed. I would never have called a man." The word *man* held disdain when she uttered it. "But with no real friends, he turned out to be the only option," she amended gently.

"And you used the video chat," Candy recalled, placing her empty plate on the coffee table and sitting back with her wine.

"Yes, and I remember how the first conversations made me so nervous." The redhead toyed with her own glass, drifting into the memory. "But Ben was easy to talk to, and I soon felt safe."

"Wow," Holly mumbled. "You've been through a great deal. And now you're ready to change."

Melody sighed heavily and her shoulders lifted in an exaggerated shrug. "No, I'm not sure that I am. But with the pandemic over, I can't hide in that place any longer." She studied Holly's delicate features intently. "He won't face-time with me forever. I will either learn to share my physical world with him, or I really will spend the rest of my life alone."

SEVEN

Genuine Concern

"ANYONE HOME?" A deep male voice from the sliding glass startled the group of women.

A look of sheer terror on Melody's countenance had Holly on her feet. Peering into the kitchen, she soothed, "It's Ben." Louder, she hollered back, "You know how to knock?"

"I used to live here, remember?" he teased, crossing the tile to join them. "It's getting late. I'm afraid I'm here to bust up the party." He smiled down at his girlfriend, her relief to see him evident.

"Well, it can't be that late," Candy started, then glanced at her watch. "Oh, it's nearly midnight." Standing, she blurted, "Are the kids in bed?"

"Hours ago," the newcomer announced. "Gary's been down over an hour. I left the back door open for you when I headed this way."

"Right," she muttered, searching under her chair for her shoes. "Sorry, we got a bit comfortable and lost track of time."

Ben winked at the owners of the house. "I'm glad things have gone so well. You must have thrown quite a celebration."

"It was all quite dignified," Mel defended, slipping on her own pumps. "Thank you, ladies, for having me."

Studying her with genuine concern, Holly nodded. "We had lots to discuss. Many stories to tell." Stepping towards her, she offered the redhead a hug. When she had her close, she whispered, "Come back any time, love."

"I will." Melody grinned broadly, giving Carol's hand a squeeze before she followed Ben to the door and out to his waiting car.

Arriving at her own dwelling a few minutes later, Candy crept into the house through the back door and avoided turning on the lights. Kicking off her shoes, she used her cell as a small torch to avoid furniture. Her movements slow, she padded quietly up the stairs and into the master bedroom, the door making a quiet click as she closed it behind her.

"I guess it went well," Gary commented from the direction of the bed.

"Oh! Ben said you were asleep."

"I'm in bed. Not really asleep," her mate corrected. Sitting up on the pliable surface, he waited for her to join him. "Are you going to tell me about it, or do I have to guess?"

Changing into her pajamas, Candy considered what she should divulge to him. She had never been the keeper of such a secret, save when Bella had confided in her about being pregnant, and she hated the idea of betraying her friend too readily. "I'm not sure that I should," she said quietly as she slid between the sheets.

"It's ok. Ben told me," he informed her gruffly. Turning his back, he pulled the covers up to his chest. "I just hope he's doing all this for the right reasons."

"What's that supposed to mean?" Candy squeaked, spooning up behind him.

"Nothing. Let's get some sleep."

His voice muffled, he sounded exhausted. Caressing the back of his head and giving his shoulder a squeeze, she quietly agreed. "I'm sorry, baby. I just wanted to be there for her."

Instantly, Gary threw back the covers and sat up on the edge of the bed. "Is this what it'll be like after you graduate, too?"

"What do you mean?" She struggled to sit up beside him, her feet not quite reaching the floor as she planted herself next to him.

"You already spend all your time locked in the office. You miss everything. Studying. Writing papers." Gary ran his fingers through his hair, giving his head a shake.

"You mean like you, being at the station at all hours of the day and night?" she snapped back, anger adding an edge to her voice. "Are we really going to do this now, with our babies asleep across the hall?" she demanded, a flattened palm indicating the nursery on the other side of their bathroom.

Breathing deeply, Gary fought down the flames in his gut. "I'm sorry, Kitten. I just feel so helpless."

"You? What does any of this have to do with you?" She stretched her arm around him, leaning against his strength. If there were a word she would never use to describe her husband, it would be helpless.

"I can't fix this," he muttered, rubbing his bare chest. "I'm a man of action. There's the fire – fight the fire. There's the wreck – pull out the victims. I don't know what to do about this." He held his hands up in frustration. "I don't see how Ben is even coping with it."

Instantly, relief flooded over her. "Is that all? Honey, you *are* helping her. By providing a safe place she can come and be surrounded by friends and family. And by giving her room. Soon enough you'll be part of her therapy, I assure you. She's going to need other men to interact with. Men besides Ben. And when that happens, you'll be on call. Like male friend duty."

Gerald chuckled. "Is that supposed to cheer me up?"

"Well, we could try making love," she cooed.

Cutting his eyes over at her, he groused, "Been into the wine, have you?"

"Only a few glasses," she confessed, pulling her feet under her and pushing onto her knees. "Of course, I could let you sleep."

"Hmm, too late for that," he growled, pushing her back and pinning her arms above her head before tucking her beneath him. "I love you so much, Candice Ford," he breathed before he pressed his lips to hers.

EIGHT

A Professional Level

"I DON'T CARE," Melody huffed to herself as she stomped through the office. "Angela!" she called loudly.

"Yes?" the young woman replied from her chair at the front desk.

"How many patients are left on the schedule?" her boss demanded crossly.

"There are four in the waiting room, with –" she paused, counting the list "— eleven more to come in before we close."

"That's too many." Melody pressed her forehead against the tips of her fingers. "Reschedule them."

Her nurse gasped. "All of them? Dr. Castleberry, are you ok?" Only a few days before Thanksgiving, reworking so many visits would be nearly impossible.

"Yes. I'm fine." Melody wafted the hand that had been supporting her, then faltered. "No, I'm not. I feel terrible. Just clear the schedule and everyone go home." Stepping into the nearest empty exam room, she closed the door and leaned her back against it.

Truth be known, she hadn't been fine in weeks. *Not since Ben sat at my table and convinced me to have dinner with the girls*, she lamented. Since then, she had thought of little else. Her secret out, she couldn't focus. Her adrenaline level high, her heart raced, and her breathing failed her. "Maybe I really am getting sick," she muttered, applying the back of her hand to her forehead.

Through the thin panel, she could hear her staff making calls. Canceling appointments on such short notice had never been done. Not in her office. But today, she had no choice. Today, she needed to get away.

Turning the knob slowly, she peeked outside. Assessing the chaos, she felt reassured none would notice her retreat. Ducking out, she strutted down the hall and made the turn to her office at the back of the suite. Once inside, she closed the door gently and contemplated the lock.

Her people well trained, she had never needed the device. No one on her staff would dare open her door unannounced, and few would attempt a knock. Her reputation matching her fiery red mane, Melody Castleberry had always been safe within those four walls, lest they feel her wrath. Despite this, she engaged the latch.

Stepping back, her eyes fixed upon it, Melody wrung her hands in front of her. Breathing deeply, she fought the panic rising within her. *In through the nose, out through a relaxed jaw*, she instructed. As her symptoms waned, she sighed.

Rounding the desk, Melody seized the straps on her purse. Throwing it over her shoulder, she jumped when a small tap of knuckles cracked against the portal. Flinging it open, she glared at the small brunette before her. "What?"

"I'm sorry, doctor," her nurse stammered. "We have two patients who can't be pushed for another week."

"Handle it." Melody held up her palm in a stopping motion, but the crease in the younger woman's brow gave her pause.

"I'm sorry. Call Dr. Martin's office and see if she can squeeze them in."

"Ms. Riley is already in the waiting room. I'll see if she can make it across town."

"Wait," Melody called as the other woman turned her back on her. "Put Ms. Riley in a room and I'll see her. But please refer anyone else and do it quickly."

"Yes ma'am," her nurse clipped as she scurried away.

Heaving a sigh, Melody dropped her bag on her desk. Tilting her head back, she continued to breathe. "One more," she whispered to herself, holding the position until the quiet rap on her door alerted her that her patient could be seen.

"Oh, my gosh." Carol gasped, allowing the front curtain to fall back into place. "Holly, guess who is sitting in our driveway!"

"Well, I know it isn't Santa," her partner teased. "It's too early for him." Before her sat Lanelle, whom she helped with a late lunch.

"It's Melody," Caroline hissed as she pulled open the front door. Stepping onto the veranda, she called, "Hey, Mel!" Seeing the other woman turn from her trek up their path, she waved. "We're all over here."

Her red curls tousled by the cool November breeze, Melody pivoted and slowly clomped across the street. To her surprise, Carol waited for her at the open portal, giving her a chance to discern who "we" might entail before she committed to entering.

"I'm sorry to bother you," she began when she arrived at the slope of their wheelchair ramp and began to climb. "I really wanted to speak to Holly."

"She's here with Lanelle," Carol pointed out, holding the door wide.

Hesitating, Melody peeked inside. "Is Gary here?"

"He's at the station," Holly called from behind her lover. "It's just us until Candy gets home from class." Arriving at the door, she beckoned, "Come in, Mel. Or do we need to go over to our place to visit?"

After a slight hesitation, Melody steeled her nerves. "Here will be fine, I guess." The girls moved to allow her inside, then closed the heavy wooden panel behind her. In the large living area, Lanelle had settled into her favorite chair and was in the process of reclining for a nap. "This is Candy's house?"

"It is," Lanelle's voice rasped as she fought with her blanket. "I never thought we'd see you here, Dr. Castleberry."

Observing the struggle, Melody caught the edge of the throw and helped her spread the cover over her legs and feet. "I know. I've put it off for so long." Giving her a slight smile, she felt calmer. "How are you doing?"

"I'm getting by," Lanelle huffed, finally able to lie still and close her eyes.

"Let's sit in the kitchen," Holly offered, indicating the arch between the two rooms.

"Yes, I need to clean before we start the next round," Caroline pointed out in a sing-song voice. "Would you like some coffee?"

"I'd love a glass of that wine," Melody countered with a short laugh. Removing her jacket, she tossed it over the back of the sofa and followed them.

"One of those days?" Holly asked, opening the fridge to oblige her. "You're in luck. This is Candy's favorite, so we always have a bottle or two on hand."

Accepting a goblet of the chilled libation, Melody sighed. "Is she at school?"

"Yes. The semester will end quickly after the holiday, and she has too many classes this fall," Carol stated succinctly.

"She's going to be a counselor," Holly added lightly, helping herself to a glass and joining their guest at the table.

"Yes, I recall her saying something about that," Melody agreed, tapping her crystal with a long nail.

"But that's not why you're here," Holly pointed out evenly.

Melody giggled. Her eyes misty, she looked up at her. "No. It's been a rough couple of weeks. I really wanted to speak to you."

Holly took a sip from her beverage, studying the other woman intently. They had more in common than the tint of their hair, and the connection drew her to her friend. "On a professional level?"

"You could say that." Melody swallowed. "I feel as if I'm coming undone."

"Have you mentioned this to your therapist?" the nurse prodded.

"I don't think she can help me with this. Not this part. Things were slower during the pandemic and that took some adjustments. Now that things are busy again, it's almost like I can't cope. As much as I felt ready for normal, now that it's here I feel overstimulated." She hesitated, studying Holly's soft green orbs. "How do you cope, as a professional? When things seem to be overwhelming."

"I changed careers," Holly replied crisply, hoisting her glass. Seeing the disbelief in Melody's eyes, she defended. "It's true! I was a hospice nurse for years, and when it began getting to me, I accepted the offer to come here. As busy as this house is, it's much quieter, and much less stressful."

"I don't think I can do that," Mel replied quietly. "I have a whole practice of patients with swelling bellies that need tending."

Holly shrugged. "I'm not suggesting you abandon your patients. Your practice is obviously important to you. Perhaps you simply need to trim back. Focus on a particular group, or just fewer of them. Something subtle could be as good a fix as something drastic."

"And my problem isn't really about my patients, is it," Melody observed, her finger continuing to tap the crystal. "The other night you seemed to understand, even on a different level."

"I've been hurt," Holly agreed, finishing the glass. "I've got the dental work to prove it." Glaring into Melody's cool stare, she didn't flinch. "You didn't say what triggered you to develop your particular phobia, and I don't care why or how it evolved. I understand it."

"Thank you," her friend whispered, dimly aware of the blonde standing at the sink. "I'm afraid my opening up to you is what brought on this episode of anxiety."

"And therein lies the question. Do you want to squash it back into its box, or are you ready to move into a bigger world?" A slight grin formed on Holly's lips. "You can't avoid men if you do. You'll have to get used to having them around more and more."

"I know." Mel's shoulders rose and fell as she sighed. "But yes, I'm ready. I just need a place I can do it while surrounded by people I trust."

Holly nodded. "We totally agree. Candy and I have discussed what we might do to help. I hope that doesn't bother you. Us talking about you behind your back."

"No, of course not." Melody blinked rapidly. "I came to you for help, so I'm relieved you care enough to have a plan. I just hope it doesn't push me too fast." She shuddered, recalling a few failed attempts from her past. "I've tried before, but it didn't work out. Maybe this time, my resolve can go the distance. With Ben to cheer me on."

"We're going to take it slow," the nurse assured. "Candy has a wealth of ideas, so we can pick and choose the ones you find appealing."

"Whatever you think, as long as it's slow." Melody grimaced. "If the choice is left up to me, I tend to fold."

Holly thought of the empty seats at past gatherings. "It won't be like that. We will begin with a series of outings for you. Small interactions with Ben, and even Gary." She watched the other woman's features intently for her response. "Is that ok?"

"I guess it'll have to be." Melody sniffed loudly, on the verge of tears. "You know I avoid public places if at all possible."

"We'll start small," Holly reiterated. "Here at the house. Maybe a car ride." She grinned, their winter schedule mentally spread before her. "We'll plan all the playdates, if you promise you'll give it your best to attend."

Mel nodded. "Thank you. If you are willing to do so, the least I can do is try."

NINE

What the Doctor Ordered

CANDY HAD BEEN tired and frustrated right up to the point of arriving home. When she noticed Melody's car in the drive across from hers, she grinned. "Exactly what the doctor ordered."

Pulling into her spot in the garage, she gathered her bags and braved the chill wind as she crossed the yard, the large metal door rolling over the stall behind her. Her heart pounding with excitement, she flung open the back door, closing it just as quickly behind her. "I'm home!"

"Hi, Candy," Melody greeted from her seat at their kitchen table. "I hope you don't mind a few guests for dinner."

"A few?" The petite blonde laughed, heading to the back of the house. "Let me drop off my books and I'll be right back." Pausing at the door of the den, she took stock of her family and their activities. Sprawled on the floor, Dakota headed up a game of woo-woos with his sister and younger brother, which apparently required a great deal of discussion on the subject on the part of Joycean.

"Go this way!" Joy pointed at the intended path. "No, Daks. Over here."

Dutiful as ever, Dakota adjusted the odd collection of items he used to construct the road, only to have Lane kick it over. Candice smiled at his persistent adjusting and gentle rebuke of the youngest Ford.

Dropping her bag, she took a knee beside them, her fingers fluffing Dakota's dark hair. "That's my sweet boy. Such a good big brother," she praised. There had been a time such actions would have warranted a tantrum. It warmed her heart to see a maturity in her eldest son she once might have thought impossible.

Turning to Joy, she added, "And such a wonderful sister. You have to help Daks with the road, don't you," she cooed, curling her daughter into a hug before scooping up her youngest son.

"I see you've found our lair," Ben teased from the doorway.

"Hey!" Candy laughed, tucking in her feet so he could join them. "I didn't realize you were here. I guess I should have known."

"Yes, I walked down after Melody texted me an hour ago. Which I may pay for later by the sounds of the gusts against the house," he lamented, indicating the swooshing noise on the exterior wall.

"An hour ago," Candice observed. "Mel didn't have patients today?"

"She sent them all home," Benjamin informed her quietly as he arranged his inventory into rows. "I'm the car lot guy," he explained.

Candy stared at his calm. "That's not like her. Melody never leaves her office until the last patient has been seen."

Ben shrugged. "Today, she couldn't take it."

"And you seem pleased about this," Candy snapped.

"I'm pleased that she came here," he soothed, his eyes darting to check the door. "She could have run home and hid in that little condo of hers. Instead, she came to her friends, and that is a big step in my book."

Watching his hands work with the toys, Candy considered his point of view. "I guess you're right."

"I think so. But go, enjoy a visit and make her feel welcome. I'll hang here with these guys until time for dinner," he suggested.

Pushing up onto his knees, he resumed his role as the car dealership. "Ok, who wants to buy a new car?"

"Me!" Joy and Daks sang in unison.

"I'll leave you to it, then." Candy found her feet and retrieved her satchel, which she placed on the office desk. Closing the door, she swore off work until both their guests had gone.

Back in the kitchen, she smiled at her mother, who appeared in the best of moods. Next to her, Melody seemed relaxed as well.

"Too bad Gary has to work," Lanelle observed as her daughter slid into the second chair on the back side of the table, also at her side.

For a moment, Melody's features crumpled before she set them back in place. "Did I say something wrong?" the matriarch asked innocently.

"I'm working my way up to that," Melody confessed, holding her grin.

"And you're here now. That's what matters," Holly concluded, joining them at the table.

Grasping her mother's hand, Candy curled their fingers together and gave it a squeeze. "Melody is coping with some issues, Mom. We'll have her over for dinner when Gary's here when she's ready."

On the other side, Melody grimaced. "That sounds odd,

doesn't it. A man avoiding his own house so a guest can be comfortable."

"He wants what's best for you, too," Candy assured. "And besides, he's working. It's not like he's staying away or anything. It just turned out this way."

Melody smiled, hiding her doubt that any of what she had said were true. They refer to their group as the bubble, which had once sounded odd to her. Now she found herself almost a part of it, with little hope or will to escape.

TEN

Dark Outside

CRANING his neck to look up at the night sky, Ben observed. "Well, at least the wind has died down."

"Yes, it's quite pleasant now," Melody agreed as she walked beside him, scarcely a foot between them.

"My lady, I do believe you have become more comfortable with me," he teased in a mock English accent, which caused her to flush in the cool evening air.

Arriving at the driveway across the street, she suppressed a grin as she looked up at him. "Thank you for seeing me to my car."

"Oh, no. This is not all," he teased, twirling his finger in the air between them. "For my next trick, I'll fetch my own vehicle and see you home."

"I couldn't ask you to do that!" She glared up at him, swallowing. "Seriously."

He didn't budge, continuing to stand over her. When the pause grew long, he pushed, "The evening is young, but it's dark out. I'd feel better if I saw you home. And maybe this time you can let me in for a bit," he suggested coaxingly.

"Ben, I have a ritual." She blinked rapidly. "Something I do when I get home, especially when it's late. I'm not sure I'm ready for you to see that part of me yet."

"I have a spare room," he offered. "The bed is made up and everything. Maybe you should just spend the night with me, more or less."

She could see the glimmer of a smile on his lips in the dim light. "You're making fun of me."

"No, but I won't sleep a wink if I don't know that you're safe." He raised a stiff digit cutting her off when she began to protest, "And no, a simple 'I'm fine' phone call won't do. Let me see you are safe, and I'll come home and sleep alone. I promise."

Melody observed the seriousness in the set of his jaw. "It means that much to you."

"You do, yes," he insisted.

"Get your car, then." She sighed, opening the driver's side to slide behind the wheel.

Not waiting to see if she changed her mind, Benjamin jogged towards home. Patting his pocket, he grinned at the fob tucked in the bottom. "I won't even have to go inside," he mused.

Climbing in, he noted her headlights waiting next to the curb. Raising a hand, he called, "I'll follow you. Just go straight home."

From her cracked window, she waved her understanding and eased her way to the corner to await his alignment behind her. "Silly man," she mumbled with an odd tightness in her gut.

It felt strange having someone, anyone, fuss over her. Leading the way, she remained calm and kept her speed down to make trailing her easier. When she pulled into her drive, she heaved a sigh of relief, until she climbed out and spied him headed up her walk.

"What are you doing?" she demanded, catching him at the door.

"I'm going to see you inside," he reminded her. "Come on, Mel. I promise not to judge."

"I can take it from here," she clipped.

"Yes, and normally I would let you. But you have me curious about this routine of yours. I'd just like to see that, and then I'll go," he suggested.

"Stubborn," she grunted, not bothering to argue. "Come in then, but I don't want to hear a word."

Opening the door, she gave it a push so that it swung wide, and she could see down the hall. Flicking on the interior lights, her hand grasped a wooden bat leaned into a corner.

"A night game?" he quipped, eyeing the device.

"Remember? It's dark outside," she mocked.

Hanging back, he grimaced. "Ok, what's next?"

"Next, we search," she replied flatly. Turning her back, she didn't wait for further questions. Veering to the right this time, she made the rounds. Arriving at the first of the two smaller bedrooms, she turned on the light and surveyed the area around the bed, then underneath, and finished by opening an empty closet.

"You do this every time you come home?" he asked, no longer joking.

"Doesn't everyone?" she mocked, moving to the next room. When she arrived at her own bedroom, she hesitated. "I'm not sure I'm ready to have you in here."

"I'll go make coffee instead," he offered.

"Coffee! I thought you were leaving," she called after him.

"Not until we talk about this," he hollered back, giving her a brief wave as he turned to make his way to the kitchen.

The brew finishing when she arrived a few minutes later, she grunted, "I won't sleep a wink tonight."

"Oh, I think you'll be fine," he countered, leaning against her sink while she located mugs.

"Did you check the pantry?" she asked in earnest.

"What exactly is it you're searching for?" He opened the door and inspected her shelves lined with canned goods, considering if a person might actually fit in the small cupboard.

"People who break into houses, of course." She didn't look at him, a warm flush creeping up her neck and staining her cheeks. "And if you're going to make fun of me, you might as well leave now and forget the coffee."

"I'm not going to poke fun," he replied gently. He closed the door and accepted his mug of brew. "Thank you."

"It helps me to feel better," she explained as she moved to her dining table and waited for him to sit opposite of her. "I don't really expect to find anything."

"That's a relief," he scoffed. "It would be a horrifying experience if you did."

"Yes, well, I've skipped it a few times and I toss and turn all night. I keep thinking, what about? It's just easier if I go look and then there's no worry," she explained in a rush.

Ben wasn't buying it, repeatedly asking himself, *how can it be like this, seeing such a ritual as normal?* Out loud, he offered, "Maybe I should sleep on your couch. Just to be sure someone hasn't hidden somewhere you missed."

"I don't need a babysitter," she mumbled.

"I'm not offering to be one. Actually, it's getting late, and —"

"And you said you would go home!" she cut him off, her voice growing shrill. "Look, Ben. You want me to trust you, I expect you to do what you say."

Stopping her with a motion of his hand, he sighed. "You're right. Let me finish this, and I'll go. Are you going into the office in the morning?"

"Yes. And I plan to make up a few appointments, so I'll be staying late," she stipulated loudly.

"Fine. Call when you get home and maybe we can face-time for a bit," he proposed gently, seeing he had upset her. "I'm sorry. I I've overstepped my bounds."

Shaking her head as she studied her cup of java, she pursed her lips, cutting her eyes up at him. "I know, you're just looking out for me."

"I am. Does that mean you'll call?" he asked anxiously, getting to his feet.

"I'll call," she agreed. Her gaze steady, she watched him place his empty cup in the sink and keep his distance as he passed her and headed for the front of the house.

"Come lock the door," he called before he disappeared into the hall.

ELEVEN

Life Was Simple

"MAN, THAT ACCIDENT WAS A ROUGH ONE," Tom observed as Gary joined him at the door of the station.

Pulling out a lawn chair and unfolding it with one hand, his hot coffee balanced in the other, his supervisor agreed. "Yes, I hate to roll up on that kind." *The no survivor kind*, he added mentally. "But we take the call," he finished, finally able to sit and enjoy the morning sun next to his long-time coworker and friend.

"We do take the call." Tom nodded slowly with a smirk. "You guys ready for the holidays? That kid of mine is going to be rotten with all the stuff my wife's bought him! And Christmas is still a month away."

"We're getting there. The house is chaos, as usual." Gary laughed at the image. "Candy will graduate with her degree this spring and things will even out."

A black Mercedes rolled by almost at a crawl, the driver obviously looking for something in the morning light. When it pulled into the lot across the street, Gerald ran his fingers roughly across his face and muttered, "Well crap."

"What, you don't want your old lady to finish?" Tom asked, then polished off his brew in a giant swig.

"No. I'm seeing a friend of the family pull up. And here he comes." Raising a hand, he indicated as Ben crossed the pavement towards them. He didn't get visitors at the station often, and when he did, they almost always meant trouble. "Don't worry, I'll take him into the office."

Standing as his family attorney and friend approached, Gary calmly folded his chair and leaned it against the others that lined the wall. "Hey, buddy," he hollered. "I'm surprised to see you hear!"

"I need a private chat." Ben didn't mince words, giving Tom a cursory nod. "Sorry to interrupt your morning," he added dolefully.

"Benjamin Monroe, this is Tom Harris," Gary introduced.

Offering his hand, Ben's features remained drawn. Standing, Tom gave it a shake, then proffered his empty cup. "I'm in need of a refill anyways. Good to meet you, though," he called over his shoulder as he shuffled to the break room and the pot that awaited him.

"I really am sorry," Ben muttered, watching him go.

"Meh, we weren't into anything important." Gary raised his hand, indicating the door to the small cubical that held his desk and other essentials. "We'll talk in there, assuming this isn't a social call."

Shaking his head, the other man lamented, "No, it isn't." Following him inside, Ben closed the door, then paused to stare at the baby refuge. Point at it, he pondered aloud, "Is that where Joy –" he stopped abruptly.

"Yes, that's it." Gary grinned at the distraction. "Four years ago, to be exact." He raised a hand, giving the contraption a fond caress. "I used to think of it as a sad thing, but now I kind of see it as hope. A second chance, if you will."

Benjamin smiled at the analogy, exhaling a tense breath. Calmer, he ran his hand through his silver-streaked hair. "You haven't even heard my dilemma and I already feel better."

"You still want to talk about it?" Gary pointed at the chair next to the door.

Pulling it forward, Ben took the seat and gathered his thoughts. When he was ready, he stated gruffly, "I followed Melody home last night to make sure she made it inside, safe and sound."

"Well, did she?" Gary teased, leaning back into his own comfortable seat.

"Of course she did." Ben hesitated, considering the events that followed. "But then she searched the entire house, bat in hand."

"A bat?" His face contorted, Gary glanced at his cup, which had gone cold.

"Yes. She keeps it near the door. Apparently, that's part of her routine. When she arrives home, she doesn't feel safe, or can't relax, until she's made sure no one has come in to hide somewhere." He shook his head slowly. "That's not normal."

"Well, we know that Melody is facing issues," Gary pointed out somberly, leaning forward onto his desk. "I guess I don't see your point."

"It scared me a little," Ben confessed. "What if this is more than she can overcome? What if we're stuck here, like this? I can't even touch her. What kind of life would that be?"

"You assumed at some point, it would just all be ok," Gary surmised, his thoughts on his own beloved. Pinching his bottom lip between a thumb and finger, he mused, "Life was sure simple before Candy came along."

"What?" Ben's brow furrowed. "What's she got to do with any of this?"

"Nothing really. I mean, at some point I was sitting exactly where you are. I was crazy about this woman, but she came with a whole bag of issues. All of us do, at some level." He leaned back in the chair thoughtfully. "I guess the real question is, can you live with Melody's bag?"

Ben scowled. "Well, I thought I could, but I'm still not sure of what all she has in it!"

"Then that's what you need to decide," Gary grunted. "You may not find out what's at the bottom for a long time. I've come to realize that I'm a rescuer." Seeing his friend's expression, he wafted a hand at him. "Never mind that. Just understand that you should only stay with this if you really love her. If you're ready to take her and her bag, if you will, no matter what's in it.

If you want to help her out of guilt or pity, walk away now. No one will think lesser of you if you do, and it would be far kinder to everyone if you are honest."

Stricken, Ben's mouth opened and closed, with no sound escaping. Had he been wrong about his own feelings? Could he make such a commitment to a woman he had never even kissed? "This isn't what I had hoped for," he bit tartly.

Gary shrugged. "It's the best I've got. I'm not the answer man. I just know what I know. We all go in hoping for sunshine and roses at the end, but we have to be prepared if it doesn't turn out that way. Especially when you know –" he stabbed the arm of the chair with a stiff digit to emphasize the unspoken words.

"Yeah, I know." Ben nodded, swallowing hard. "I do love her. I couldn't even sleep last night, thinking about this. I need to have her closer to me. I feel so helpless, with her across town. It used to be enough, seeing her on that little screen, but now I just want more."

"You can't push her, Ben. I've been there, and you have to let it all unfold as it should," Gary stated firmly. "It'll be complicated and messy. It may even be painful. Like I said, you have to know your reasons. And then you have to stick to them."

"I'll give it a good think then, and let you know. Or let her know." Ben chuckled at the blunder. "I guess she's the one I need to be talking to."

"She is," Gary seconded, getting to his feet. "But I'll be here if you need me."

"Thanks." Rising, Ben offered his hand, then pulled him into a hug with a slap on the back before he opened the door to leave. "It's good to have friends she and I can both count on."

"You know you do," Gary assured, showing him to the exit.

TWELVE

A Nice Tradition

"WHAT'S ALL THIS?" Melody asked as Ben's Mercedes eased into the parking area behind the Ford house.

"This is a tradition," Ben replied cryptically. Climbing out, he skipped around the front and opened her door, guiding her out into the afternoon sun.

From the house, bags and boxes were being carried out and placed in the back of Gary's Suburban. "It looks like grocery shopping in reverse," she observed.

Dropping off her load, Candy strolled over to greet them. "Caroline started it during the pandemic. Now we do it on purpose. This is our third year," she boasted. Sidling up beside her, she added quietly, "We'd like to invite you to ride over with us."

"And what exactly is it?" Melody persisted, growing annoyed at their non-answers.

"It's for the foodbank," Ben said quietly, leaning close enough to smell her shampoo-fresh curls. "Each shopping trip, everyone buys a few extra cans during the year, and we save them. Then we deliver them to the shelter downtown just in time for the holidays."

Spying Gerald, Melody stiffened. "That's a nice tradition," she managed, her eyes following as he checked the load and closed the doors.

"Will you ride over with us?" Candy grasped the redhead's arm with both hands to offer her support. "The guys can sit up front and we can take the back."

"I'd like to sit by Ben, if that's ok," Melody suggested.

Surprised that she had consented to the outing so quickly,

he agreed wholeheartedly. "Sure, we can take the back,"

Climbing in, Gary got out of the way so they could enter and claim their seats, noting that his wife took her usual one next to him. "They good back there?" he asked covertly, indicating the couple behind them with a nod over his shoulder.

"It's what she wanted," Candy whispered with a grin.

Adjusting his mirror, Gary expertly reversed around the curve and down the drive. When he had cleared it, and sat in the street, he moved the shifter to drive and slowly rolled away. "It's quite a haul this year," he observed loudly.

"Are they expecting you?" Melody asked, her eyes fixed on the man's head in the seat in front of her.

"Yes, they'll give us some help to unload," he replied jovially.

Glancing at her profile, Benjamin sighed. "So close, and yet so far," he muttered under his breath, grateful she had agreed to the outing.

When they arrived at the mission, Gary backed into the designated spot and climbed out. "Would you like to come in?" he offered to no one in particular.

"I'm fine," Melody croaked, sliding a little towards the center of the bench seat and closing the gap between her and Ben. His hand resting on the leather, she laid hers over the top and squeezed.

Electric shocks radiated from the point of contact, stealing his breath and curling his toes. "Baby?" he whispered when her grip tightened.

Her head turning slowly, Melody gasped for air. When their eyes met, she whimpered.

"Easy, love," he soothed, pulling his hand free and turning it to clasp hers, locking their fingers together palm too palm.

In the cargo space behind them, a few workers reversed the process they had witnessed previously. In a matter of minutes, the stockpile had been removed and the massive doors closed.

As soon as they shut, Melody panted, squealing, "Oh, my God."

Pivoting to look at her, Candy noticed the panic on her friend's flushed cheeks, than the hand wrapped in the gloved fingers beside her. Lifting her chin, she avoided staring at their connection, and instead made a show of watching her husband speak to one of the volunteers. "I think I'm going to go listen," she announced, practically leaping from the vehicle and closing the door with a slam.

"Are you ok," Ben asked as soon as she had gone.

"I'm terrified." Melody squirmed, remaining in his grasp. "But I'm ok. You knew we were coming here," she accused, her eyes narrowed.

"I knew they were. You were given the option, remember?" he teased. His thumb scraped gently across the backs of her fingers, only detecting them slightly through the material between them. "This is nice," he added, tapping them lightly.

Melody's smile spread slowly, her bright red hair framing her face from the edges of her cap. "I think that's first base," she mocked, her anxiety hidden for the moment.

"It's something," he breathed, his tongue flicking out to wet his lips in anticipation. But her smile relaxed, and he knew that would be the extent of their contact, at least for the time being.

As if on cue, the vehicle's owners returned to claim their seats. "Who wants ice cream?" Gary cajoled.

"Me," Candy sang, glancing to see the couple still maintained their grip on each other as she pulled her seatbelt into place.

Melody's voice quavered, "Do they have a drive thru?"

"Uh, I don't think so," Gary admitted sheepishly, as if apologetic he had suggested it. "Maybe we should pass," he offered, noting the pout on his wife's lips. "Sorry, Kitten."

Melody's jaw tightened, her frustration with the situation taking a slow boil. "I can get out."

Benjamin's head pivoted, his eyes snapping to meet hers. "Are you sure?"

"I've let this thing run my life long enough," she whispered hoarsely, adjusting her fingers to tighten their grasp. "I think I at least need to try."

"Ok, let's have some ice cream," Ben voiced loudly to their driver in agreement. From the angle, he could see the satisfied smirk on his friend's features, and he briefly wondered what else they had planned.

Arriving at the small local parlor a few minutes later, Candy and Gary climbed out to wait at the door for the other couple. Leaning over, Gary murmured, "Do you really think she's ready for this? I'd hate to see a meltdown in the middle of the creamery."

"Holly thinks that she is," Candy huffed, crossing her arms across her chest to combat the cold. "I can't believe she's moving so fast." Looking through the glass, she grinned. "At least there's no crowd. If we hurry, it'll just be us and the clerk inside."

Opening and holding the door so Mel and Ben could pass through, Gary smiled down at the doctor. "Hang in there," he muttered as she slipped past, which only increased her speed.

"Oh," Melody gasped once inside. "I don't think I've ever been here." Her eyes wide, she took in the long, L-shaped counter filled with frozen delights. Shuffling slowly, she held Ben's gloved hand between both of hers as she pulled him along. "Which is the best?" she mused loudly.

"Yes," he replied covertly, earning a dark glance. "Hey, I like ice cream," he mocked. "Any and all." He smiled at the clerk and ordered his cup. "I'll take a triple scoop Sunday with the works."

The young man appeared bored by the process. "What flavors?"

"Surprise me," Ben suggested. "Anything with chocolate in it."

Her eyes fixed on the procedure, Melody hissed, "Do you know how many calories that is?"

"Today, it doesn't matter," Benjamin teased. Accepting the treat with his free hand, it pained him that he would have to release her to enjoy it. "I should have gotten a cone."

Seeing his dilemma, she grinned up at him. "I'll have the same."

When they were all served, Gary presented his card for payment. "Are we eating them here?" A man with a group of children entered as he asked, making the decision for them. "I guess not. We can sit in the car," he suggested instead.

"Good idea," Candy seconded, leading their friends out the door.

Back in the Suburban, Melody breathed easier. "Thank you for your understanding." She used her spoon to sample a bit of the topping in an effort to hide her rising trepidation.

Closing his door firmly, Gerald probed in a relaxed tone, "Does this mean we can officially count on you for our holiday dinner this year?"

Candy appeared stricken at the thought of their chaotic

Christmas mornings. "Gary! We're taking small steps. Our house might be a bit much, at least for this year."

Melody's hand trembled, vibrating her spoon as she considered the offer. "I have to agree with Candy. I'll keep coming around though, for treats like these," she joked.

Ben ate his slowly, aware her mood had shifted once again, hesitation replacing her bravado. "It's weeks away, love. We'll have more chances to practice," he assured.

Melody swallowed a bite of creamy deliciousness, glancing at him dolefully and wishing it were that simple.

THIRTEEN

Pretty Tough

"I TRIED. I'M NOT READY." Melody glanced at Benjamin's relaxed frame as he leaned against the corner between the living room and hall. "Go without me."

Ben shook his head slowly. "There's no point in going without you," he reminded gently. "Roger and Eve are coming to meet you."

"I don't give a damn why they're coming," she seethed, her face flushed to match her amber waves.

"You don't mean that," he argued as gently as he could, marveling at how quickly he had learned to control his own rushes of emotion. He knew in good time, she would as well. "Come on, baby."

Mel glowered at the hand he raised in offer to her. "No," she grunted, her nosed scrunched at the memory of holding it tightly only a few days before. "You're confusing me," she hissed.

A chime sounded in his pocket, and Ben withdrew the device. "They are going to hold dinner until we get there," he announced casually. She made a beautiful target in her holiday attire, and he cautiously aimed for the right spot. "You're all dressed. I'm all dressed up. Let's go and at least make an appearance. If you can't sit down with them, we'll take another room. The office or the den." The Ford house was filled with rooms she could retreat too if she needed to.

"Why can't I just say no!" she huffed, stamping her heel against the kitchen tile.

Straightening himself, Benjamin moved across the carpet, closing the distance between them. "You agreed to come," he soothed. "These are last minute jitters."

Melody ground her teeth. "Stay back," she warned.

Pausing his step, mere feet to go, he breathed, "I'm not going to hurt you."

The attack came without warning, her hands flailing when she laid into him. Her nails sharp, a deep scrape marked his cheek. She squealed, slapping and punching at his masculine features.

"Mel, stop!" he commanded, his fingers curling around her wrists to confine them. Holding tightly, one in each hand, a trickle of blood rolled from his nostril onto his upper lip. He let it drip, refusing to release her.

Jarred from her rage at the sight of the bright red splotch it formed on his white shirt, she gasped. "Oh, God. I'm so sorry!"

"Can I let go now?" he bit tartly.

"Of course!" Yanking her arms free, she fumbled for a dish-towel. "Here. I'll get some ice."

"Just sit," he commanded, snatching the cloth and opening the ice bin for himself.

Tears on her cheeks, Melody obliged. Glancing at her, Ben held his anger at bay. *Gary warned me this wouldn't be easy*, he silently recalled, her bag full of nasty surprises. Folding a few cubes inside the material, he pressed it against the bridge of his nose and stemmed the flow.

A guilty expression darkening her features, Melody lamented, "We can't go now. You have blood on your shirt."

"I'll wear the jacket," he countered evenly, inspecting the stain. "It'll cover it fine."

"You don't give up, do you," she sniveled.

"Call me stubborn." He raised his free hand, indicating the door. "Get your coat, and let's not make our friends wait any longer."

"Is that a black eye?" Gary hissed when the two men were alone in his kitchen.

"Mel," Benjamin clipped. "She needed a bit of convincing to get here."

Gary gaped at him. "You didn't."

"Force her? Pfft, no." Ben shook his head, glancing around at the empty space, Candy and Carol having whisked her into the living area as soon as they arrived. He pursed his lips thoughtfully. "She attacked me." He could see the disbelief in his friend's eyes and added, "I got too close, I guess. I grabbed her hands to stop her, but it was the blood that did the trick." He sneered, tracing the line of his nose. "She's pretty tough."

"I bet," Gary coughed, glancing at the archway between them. "Mom and Dad are waiting in the den for an introduction. Do you think we're safe to bring them out?"

"What are you guys whispering about?" Holly asked, closing Lanelle's door behind her as she joined them.

"We're deciding a few things," Gary covered smoothly.

Not buying it, Holly stared up at her former roommate. "She got violent," she surmised.

"Only a little." Ben shrugged. "I didn't think anyone would notice. She didn't hit me that hard."

The nurse frowned. "Only if they don't look at you. We need to rethink our seating arrangements."

"Well, we can't do the porch," Ben quibbled. "I saw flurries on the drive over."

"Lanelle and the children have already eaten," Holly detailed. "It's nap time for all of them, so that will give us some room. Four couples can sit around the dining room table comfortably."

"Let's bring out Eve and Roger. If she tolerates the living room –" Gary stopped short as his father's lanky form shuffled past the arch.

In the front room, Melody sat stiffly in Lanelle's favorite chair next to a roaring fire. Her gaze fixed on the bubble's eldest member, she gripped the armrest tightly. "Hello, Mr. Ford," she whispered.

"Call me Roger," he replied in his gravelly tones. He paused, keeping the ottoman between them. "Can we eat now?" he called to his son. "My old belly's picked up quite a rumble."

Gary looked his father up and down, having never seen him appear so frail. "Sure, pops." He indicated to Candy to join him, then suggested, "We should spread out in the dining room and start the meal. Melody and Ben can join us when she's ready."

Seeing the attorney's injuries for the first time, Candy glared at him. She had meddled in the lives of others plenty of times, but this could be the worst outcome she had ever seen. "That's fine. Caroline, can you serve the meal?" Grasping her father-in-law's arm, she guided him to the back of the house with a bit of fear twisting her gut at what might happen next.

FOURTEEN

Eve Advice

THREE OF THE four couples ate quietly in the dining room when Ben and Melody entered to join them. Their seats closest to the door, he placed his girlfriend at the head of the table, with Candy on the far side providing a buffer between her and Gary.

"You tricked me," Melody accused. Her green eyes narrowed into thin slits, she studied the crafty old man seated at the far end opposite her. Eveline to his right, between him and their son, he appeared far less decrepit than he had only a few minutes before.

"Not necessarily," Roger mused. "I simply made myself less menacing." He grinned knowingly at the younger woman. "It's good to finally have you inside the bubble," he welcomed.

"Hmpf," Eve grunted. "After all the times her chair has sat empty, it's a miracle she's here."

"Mother," Gary warned in a low tone.

"Don't 'mother' me!" Eveline snapped. "You said she was terrified of men." She indicated their family attorney and friend seated next to the redhead. "Why is he the one who looks like he's been pummeled?"

Melody flicked her gaze around the group, it finally landing

77

on her escort. "I'm sorry. I had a difficult time before we left the house," she justified coolly.

"That's no excuse," Eve berated. "I think our family has endured a great deal on your behalf. Benjamin is completely smitten with you. You have no right or excuse to treat him so poorly."

"Mother, I don't think dressing her down in front of everyone is going to help," Gary pointed out sternly.

"No, she's right," Melody defended, her fingers toying with the linen napkin she had placed in her lap. "I should never have hit him." She bit her lower lip to prevent the tremor that warned of tears.

Instinctively, Ben reached for her hand under the maple top, a moment of panic twisting his gut as his fingers curled around it. A wave of relief quickly forced it aside when she accepted the gesture. "We're making progress," he upheld valiantly.

"Don't enable her," Eve warned, unmoved by the display.

"Eveline," Roger groaned. "Can anything happen in this family without you having to hand out unsolicited advice?"

"No," she clipped, dropping her utensils to lean against her folded hands, purposely placing her elbows on the flat surface before her. "As the head of the family, it is my duty to say my piece."

Benjamin grinned at being referred to as family. "Thank you, Mrs. Ford. It's nice to see you are as feisty as ever."

"Flattery will get you nowhere," she warned, waggling a finger at his girlfriend. "You, young lady, need a swift kick in the pants."

Directly across from her, Holly gasped. "Eve! You can't speak to her that way! She has a condition!"

"I can and I will," the older woman countered. "What she has is a need to accept the good things she has around her." Eve sniffed loudly, her blue orbs darting between the shocked expressions. "All your coddling. I believe in mind over matter." The noise of small feet padded across the ceiling above them, bringing her sharp tone into check. "If you put your mind to it, whatever happened in the past won't matter," she finished with a grin. "Now, I believe my grandson is ready for some grammy time." On her feet, Eve had gone to collect Lane before the others could stop her.

"Wow," Benjamin breathed. "Her fiery spirit never seems to diminish."

"Surely she isn't implying I should just get over it," Melody snapped, squeezing his digits to the point of pain.

"That's exactly what she's suggesting," Roger soothed. "But we lived in a different time," he defended. "Before shrinks and meds. Back when people simply had to deal with things and do exactly that. Get over them."

"Get over them," Holly huffed the echo. "As if that would work."

"Well, I can't say that it did, but people seem to be a lot more sensitive with a lot more 'conditions' these days," he rebuked. "Back then, we didn't have time to wallow in… things." The word fell flat across the silent table.

"Thanks, Dad," Gary grumbled, glancing uncomfortably at his wife.

"I don't know," Candice whined with a shrug. "I like to think I've come a long way with my own struggles, and I have to admit that things really didn't change for me until I got my attitude in line." She smiled at the woman next to her. "Either way, just know that this circle—" she used a finger to indicate the ring surrounding the table "– we're here for you. For as long as it takes."

Melody blinked at her, the tear she had been blinking at trickling over to streak down her cheek. "I'm so sorry that I hit you." She swiped at the drop of sorrow, not daring to look at him. She couldn't imagine a time she would have stayed in that seat, enduring their stares. "I guess I really have changed."

Still holding her other hand firmly, Ben scowled. "Because I pissed you off to the point of violence?"

"No, silly." She managed a small grin. "Because I haven't leapt out up and run for the car. Or the street. I'm actually quite good at being pissed." She bit her bottom lip. "Since I was a little girl people have said that my attitude matches my hair."

"A knock at redheads," he lamented with her.

"Yes. It was one tactic I could count on to keep people away from me when I wanted to be left alone. But not you." She used her free hand to trace the line of his jaw, her thumb gliding over the deep cut her nail had left in his cheek. "I would promise it will never happen again, but I'm not sure yet that I'm ready to call my anxiety beaten. Or the tantrums that come with it."

"It's ok. I'll know next time to duck." Ben laughed loudly as the others joined him for a brief moment of levity before he sighed, and the group fell quiet. "I guess we might as well eat. I mean, the meal looks fantastic," he praised indicating their plates to the housekeeper on his other side.

"Aww, thanks," Caroline moaned, her cheeks taking on a faint pink hue. "You enjoy, and I'll go plate the dessert."

FIFTEEN

Get Over It

"HAPPY ANNIVERSARY," Caroline hummed to the girl seated on the far side of their breakfast table.

"Dang it!" Candy snapped, then laughed. "Why do I always forget?"

"Because it's Christmas Eve, and that's far more important than little old us," Gary teased, sliding into the chair beside her. Wafting his phone at her before laying it beside him, he added, "That was Ben. They've had a rough week, but he and Melody will definitely be joining us for the winter festival downtown."

Clasping her hands together, Holly squeaked, "Oh, how delightful!"

"Yes, but they're going to bring his car," Gary continued. "That way, if she has a meltdown, they'll be able to leave."

"That and we are about out of room," Candy observed, counting family members.

"A nice problem to have," Lanelle slurred, smiling at her daughter's fuss.

"Agreed." Candy dropped her arm across her aged shoulders and squeezed. "And actually, I'm going to take my car as well. The kids can ride with me, while you and the girls can ride in the van with your wheelchair. I think there will be room for Gracie's car seat. What time are they meeting us?"

"At five," Gary supplied, filling his plate with bacon and eggs from the platter before them. "But that's just an estimate. We'll get there when we get there, and so will they."

"I'm just glad you were able to have the day off together," Caroline said with a bit of sass. She glared at her employer, waiting for her to acknowledge the jab.

But Candy played it cool. "Me too. I didn't realize how much work a mid-winter course would be!"

"And you really graduate now in May." Holly soothed the tiff between them.

"Yes," Candy hissed, grinning at their nurse. "As long as I pass all my classes with a C or better, I get to walk the stage."

"C's get degrees," Gerald concluded. Leaning over, he kissed his mate on the forehead. "We'll be proud of you, either way, Kitten."

Hours later, Candy had just placed Lane in his stroller when Ben's black Mercedes eased into the empty space next to her compact car. "Hold Joy's hand, Daks," she instructed, glancing to see who had taken the spot. "Oh, Mel!" she gasped as the doctor stepped out onto the fresh snow.

"I know. Amazing we're on time, right?" Melody grinned at her friend anxiously. "Actually, I've been employing some recent advice, and it appears to be working." She glanced at her boyfriend, who only nodded. "Well, most of the time."

"And what advice is that?" Candy asked absently, still getting her children in line for the walk up to the entrance gate.

"I'm doing my best to get over it. I mean, I thought I was doing that before, but now even more so. Mind over matter." The red hair peeking out around the edge of her knit cap framed her features perfectly as she smiled at Dakota and offered him her hand.

Staring at it, the eldest blinked a few times, then placed his gloved fingers into hers, his other still firmly holding Joycean. "Horsies, Joy," he sang.

"Yes, we have money for the horses," Candy agreed, ready to give the carriage a push. Closing her hatchback, she smiled at their connection. "Are you walking with Auntie Mel-Mel?"

"Mel-Mel," he repeated, pulling them to increase their pace.

"How about if I carry Joy?" Ben offered, bending to scoop her into his arms.

"That might be a good idea," Melody agreed, holding her charge firmly. "This ground may be slick for little feet."

Placing Joy on his hip, he cradled her with one arm and dropped the other to catch Mel's free hand. "Walk between us," he suggested, eyeing the crowd on the other side of the fence.

"It's beautiful," she replied, also taking in the view. As the sun set, the bright lights of the path took on a festive glow that called to her. "I've missed so much, locking myself away all this time."

"We come every year," Candy informed them airily. Working to keep the stroller moving, she sighed. "I love this thing most of the time, but days like this, not so much."

"Is that Lanelle?" Melody asked as she indicated a speeding chair coming down the frozen walk.

"I'm afraid that it is." Candice grimaced. "She's going to hurt herself on that thing someday."

"It's not as fast as it looks," Ben challenged, dropping Mel to give Lane a shove. "Where's Gary? He's the muscle around here, he should be pushing this thing."

Spying his father and the girls, Dakota cackled. "Daddy!"

A few moments later, the groups converged, to everyone's relief. Gary took over the stroller and Candy claimed Daks. Carol and Holly hadn't bothered with one for Grace, and took turns carrying her in her warm snuggie; basically a tiny sleeping bag with a hood.

"Are we set now?" Candy asked, already exhausted. "We haven't even made it through the gate." Glancing at Melody, she paused, then turned to Ben. "You better let me take Joy. Mel is going to need a strong arm to lean on once we get inside."

"I have to agree," he replied, handing the girl over and reclaiming the doctor's hand. "What if we hang back a bit?"

"No!" Melody blurted, her eyes on the hoard of people wandering through the outdoor garden. "I want to stay with the group."

"She's safer with us," Holly agreed, falling into step beside her. "Let us know if you need to stop for a timeout," she advised.

Once they had paid for their tickets, the party tromped along with Melody floating near the center. Never leaving her side, Ben kept one eye on the passersby, and the other on her, which seemed to work for a while, at least. But eventually, they each wanted to visit a different attraction, leaving them with little choice but to strike out on their own.

"You should go," Ben pointed out directly. "Melody and I will take it slow. And we'll text if we decide to leave."

Watching them scatter, Melody clung to his arm. "I didn't know having a family could take so much energy," she observed as Gary and Candy wrangled their herd along the busy walk.

"Yes, I've often thought the same thing," Ben agreed with a chuckle, then turned his attention to her. "Are you really ok?"

"Just don't lose me," she warned. "I haven't been in such a crowded place in years."

Moving steadily, almost as a single unit, the couple made their way down to the garden entrance, then turned onto the gravel path. "I love all the lights," she breathed, still wary of those who passed them. "I wish we could be the only ones here."

"But Christmas is for sharing," he reminded her gently. Seeing a rest spot off to the side, he guided her towards it. "Let's have a breather. I wouldn't sit on the wooden bench, but we can at least get away from the throng for a moment."

Melody giggled, relieved at his suggestion, but at that moment a couple of loud chaps brushed against her. Her smile eliminated, she froze. Lifting her chin, she stared up at the burly bearded one who hung back to tower over her.

"Hey there, cutie," he clipped, flashing a toothy grin.

"Excuse us," Ben intervened. Pulling her arm, he pivoted her stiff form to wedge himself between them. "She's with me," he snarled once he had her behind him.

"No sweat." The pair grumbled a few words to each other, then continued down the path.

Shoving Melody towards their chosen haven, Ben glowered down at the soggy seat. Thinking quickly, he removed his jacket and dropped it over, the exterior facing down so they could sit on the warm, fuzzy inside.

"There you go, baby," he soothed as she sank down beside him. Glancing at her, he could see she was all funned out. "Aww, I'm sorry they startled you."

"I'm ok." Her voice quavered, giving her away.

"You're not, but we'll sit here for a few minutes and see if it helps," he offered.

Pulling her stocking cap off and freeing her curls, she held it out to him. "Put this on your head. It'll keep you warmer now that you don't have your coat."

"Does that really work?" he asked, stretching the knit material into place.

"I'm a doctor. Yes, it works." She laughed, grateful for his distraction. "Hypothermia isn't really funny."

"We won't stay long," he assured, rubbing his hands together briskly and eyeing her fluffy coat. "Too bad there isn't room in there for both of us."

Curling her tongue, Melody considered the situation. "I think you'll be ok with the cap. When we go again, I'll try harder not to run into anyone."

"They did it on purpose," he growled.

Her brow furrowed. "Why?"

"A lovely little redhead, why wouldn't they?" he teased.

Staring up at him, the crinkles slowly faded. "You think I'm lovely?" she breathed, her mind on all the trouble she had brought him.

"I think you're gorgeous," he replied crisply, leaning slightly towards her.

"But I'm such a mess." Her chin dimpled. "I can't even walk through a Christmas display by myself."

"That's ok. I've got you. Remember?"

"Oh, no!" she gasped, her eyes darting around them. "We have to go!"

"Go? Why?" he joined her search, then turned his attention back to her delicate features. "Are you going into panic mode?"

"No, silly! It's starting to snow!" She held up a gloved palm and a few flakes landed on it, as if to demonstrate her point.

"Good. Maybe some of these guys will head inside and we'll get to walk through here more or less alone after all." He tossed his chin, indicating those who had picked up their pace on the path before them.

"What a wonderful plan," she breathed, drawn to the sparkle in his eyes. "But seriously, we need to get your jacket back on soon."

He stared at her satiny pink lips. "What?"

"I said, you need to get warm."

"Ok." He leaned forward, pausing a breath away from her

and whispered, "I'm so in love with you, Melody. I'm always warm when I'm around you."

Her heart thumping inside her chest, she lifted her face to meet his attempt, her lips parting when they brushed against his.

Only a few seconds, the kiss lingered between them for what seemed an eternity before he finally broke the connection. "Was that ok?" he croaked.

"I think so," she replied in her own dazed state. "Let me check." She closed her eyes, returning to the kiss.

When the connection ended for the second time, he laughed. "Man, it's really coming down." He used a gloved hand to swipe a few flakes out of her hair. "Seriously, we can make out later. Right now, we need to go."

On his feet, he indicated for her to join him, then presented her with her cap. Standing, she worked it back into place and smoothed her hair while he buttoned his coat.

"You're right, most seem to be headed inside," she observed.

"Good." He reached for her hand and guided her onto the path. "We'll keep to the right and see the sights. A little snow never hurt anyone," he teased with glee.

"We should have snagged a hot beverage on the way out," she observed, noting a few held large cups of steaming brew.

"We'll get one when we get back inside," he agreed.

Following the path, they enjoyed each of the glowing displays. Holding his arm, Melody lingered at each, drawing out their time together as long as she could. However, after an hour they were completely chilled, and she finally admitted it was time to head back inside.

When they had completed the loop, they were relieved to find the snack bar still had coffee. Able to remove his gloves, Ben opened his phone and then groaned. "Looks like we've outlasted the rest of the group. They are all headed to the girls' place to load up the fireplace and have a little dinner."

"You want to go join them?" Melody asked, calmly sipping her hot liquid.

Grinning at her, Benjamin considered the suggestion. "You've come a long way. You don't even seem nervous."

"I told you, I hide it well," she challenged. "But yes, I do feel calmer. I don't know I could have attempted such an outing without you." Her gaze distant, she added, "What if we went back to my place instead."

"Time to check the closets?" he mocked.

The air tight in her chest, she breathed, "I can't do this if you tease me."

Frowning, he glared at her. "Do what?" he pushed. "Don't get my hopes up if you're not serious."

"I don't know what I am," she admitted quietly. "But if you'll go home with me, we can light a fire of our own and see where it leads."

SIXTEEN

Duty and Devotion

DRIVING CAREFULLY in the fresh snow, Ben fought the urge to push his speed to get to her place. He'd been with his share of women, but he couldn't remember a single one of them at the moment. Glancing at her profile, he sighed; he only had eyes for her.

Pulling to the curb in front of her townhome, he commanded, "Wait for me. I don't want you taking a fall."

Smiling, she nodded. Obediently staying put, she accepted his hand once the door had been opened and he guided her onto the curb.

"It's slick," he pointed out, maintaining his grip on her as they navigated the path.

"I've walked on snow before." She giggled, pleased with the heavy warmth of his protective arm draped across her shoulders. Applying the key and opening the portal, she hung back as he pushed her aside to enter before her, then followed.

As soon as the door closed and their coats had been removed, Benjamin took charge of the bat. Leading the way to the right, they made her routine search together. Only this time he was all business.

Watching him from the door of the first bedroom, as if inspecting her trainee, Melody grinned as he checked the closet and under the bed. In the second room, he even peeked behind the long curtains that covered the window. "Very thorough," she approved.

"Thanks. I believe your room is next," he suggested, still wielding the wooden device. Brandishing it as he opened her chamber, he flicked on the light and paused to take it all in. He then went straight across to the closet, followed by the door next to it. "Nice colors," he observed, once the master bath had been cleared. "I really like the size of that tub."

"Yes. It's a wonderful place to relax," she agreed, noting his stance. "I didn't think any of this was necessary," she pointed out gruffly.

"It makes you happy," he explained with a shrug.

"Such duty and devotion," she praised, smiling up at him. Standing close, she leaned towards him, and he lowered his lips to hers.

When the connection ended, Melody sighed. "Ben, I have something else I probably should tell you." Her wide green eyes fixed on his, her voice quavered. "I've never."

He stared at her, waiting for the rest. When it didn't come, he leaned back, putting some distance between them. Applying his palm and fingers to roughly massage his chin, he mumbled, "I see. I didn't figure that you had, to be honest. And I can't guarantee that you will tonight."

"What do you mean?" She scowled, retreating to put another foot between them. Looking him up and down, she spat, "I thought we came here to make love."

"We are making love," he breathed. "Every moment I'm with you is like heaven." He grazed her cheek with the backs of his fingers as he sauntered past.

Taking the hallway, Ben crossed the living area with

purpose. In the kitchen, he opened the pantry to find no one there. "All clear in here," he called. Turning to her refrigerator, he opened it casually to peer inside. "Do you want to start the fire, or shall I?"

Melody glared at him from her position next to the dinette, then marched around to the hearth. Lighting the ceramic logs, she mumbled to herself. Once the fire blazed, she sat back on her haunches to find a glass of wine hanging next to her ear. Looking up slowly, his masculine features smiled down at her, softening her disgust.

"Thank you," she muttered. Accepting the crystal once she had regained her feet, she sighed.

"Don't be so glum," he instructed, indicated the sofa.

"I'm not glum," she rebuked. "I just put myself out there, and you shut me down."

"I haven't shut anything down," he teased, taking a cushion and draping his free hand along the back. "I'm savoring."

"Do you savor all the girls?" She sat with the far arm of the couch pressing against her hip, so the tips of his fingers could almost reach her.

He hesitated, his lip toying with his goblet. "Only the ones I intend to marry."

Her jaw dropped and Melody gaped at him. Her chest in a conundrum, she couldn't tell which was worse; her heart pounding against her ribs or her lungs gasping for air. "You didn't just propose to me."

"No," he clipped, stretching his fingers to test the distance. "But I think you should know I'm not in this for the sex." He grinned at her, unable to control his giddy restlessness.

"What if it's not any good?"

"I bet it'll be fine." He sipped his wine noisily, turning to gaze at the dancing flames. "You make a nice fire."

"Are you playing hard to get?" She sounded annoyed, her tongue tracing the edges of her teeth.

"I'm not the one that took the far end of the couch," he mocked.

Pivoting, she placed her glass on the table behind his arm, next to one of the figurines. Pulling herself across the fabric, she relieved him of his and pressed herself against him as she set it on the table next to hers. Her heart still thumping loudly in her ears, she pushed a leg over to straddle him with his emptied hand resting on her folded hip.

His legs sandwiched between hers, she had never felt so vulnerable, and yet so in control. She whispered, her lips brushing against his ear as she nuzzled him, "Is this how you do it?"

"It's one way," he slurred. Slowly pulling his extended arm in, his fingers worked their way up her back and threaded into her hair. Finding her scalp, he massaged it gently. The hand on her leg squeezed her thigh, and he groaned, letting her take him as far as she wanted to go.

SEVENTEEN

As Christmas Goes

CANDY AWOKE to near darkness early Christmas morning. Inhaling deeply, she breathed out in a long, satisfied sigh. Rolling onto her side, she stretched out her arm, reaching for her husband. But instead of his muscled frame, she found only cold sheets and a crumpled blanket on his side of the mattress.

"Damn," she muttered to herself. Sitting up straight, she stretched, then studied the window that faced their back yard. Through it, not a hint of daylight troubled the dark sky peeking through the barren trees.

Throwing back her covers, Candice didn't waste time on a shower. No, she would need to move quickly if she were to stay ahead of her beloved children on such a magical morning.

Opting for jeans and a holiday sweater, she only primped long enough to brush her teeth and bring order to her honey-gold hair. Then, she slipped out in stocking feet and made a beeline for the stairs. Not daring to peek on any of her sleeping brood, she made it to the bottom floor with nary a sound to disturb them.

Gary snorted a sleepy greeting when she arrived in the

living room to find him stretched in her mother's favorite chair. "Gary," she hissed, giving his foot a shake.

"Hmph, what?" He smacked his lips a few times and squinted an eye to look at her.

"Is everything finished?" She could see the rows of toys he had been assembling when she made her way up to their room the night before. "They look good, honey."

"Remind me never to buy bikes and doll houses in the same year again," he grunted while fighting to turn on his side. "Are they up?"

"No. And I didn't peek, so we will have more time as long as we are quiet. I'll start the coffee and see when everyone else will get here," she informed him with a shake of her head. "Are you going to sleep a little longer?"

"No, I smell horrid. I'll go shower and be down after," he lamented.

However, he didn't move, and she decided to let him be. Going into the kitchen, she opened her cell to call the girls first. "Hey, Carol! Merry Christmas." She busied herself with the brew while they chatted.

"Good morning," Carol sang in return. "Is everything jumping over there yet?"

"No, I'm the only one up so far. How long before you guys arrive?" Closing the lid and starting the device, she added, "Did Eve and Roger make it over?"

"They did, and they are raring to go. I'd say thirty minutes or less," her housekeeper informed her. "Grace is in a good mood, so we want to let her open gifts and get some pictures before we go."

"Sounds wonderful," Candy agreed. "I'm making the coffee, and we'll have snack breakfast later. Do you need me to do anything prep-wise for the dinner?"

"No, I have it all set. I'll put it in the oven when I get there, and we'll be ready to eat by twelve."

"You are amazing," her boss praised. "We'll be ready when you get here."

Ending the call, Candy scrolled down and located her next contact, Benjamin Monroe. Listening to it ring, she wondered if Melody would actually feel like joining them. Things had seemed to go well the night before, at the winter festival, and she hoped it had not been too much of a good thing.

"Hello?" Ben's voice rasped.

"Hey! It's Candy!" she greeted. "Are you coming down?"

Silence. Then muffled sounds of commotion before he whispered, "I'm not at home. It'll be a while before we make it over."

Candy's heart stopped for an instant, then skipped a few beats with joy. She dared in a hoarse whisper, "Are you at Mel's place?" Her eyes darted around anxiously to see if anyone else might hear.

More silence. Then he said simply, "Candy. Yes, we'll go later. I'm telling her."

At that point, Candice realized he no longer spoke to her. "Hey, it's ok. We'll be opening presents in about an hour, and dinner will be noonish. You guys come when you can."

Not waiting for a reply, she ended the call abruptly, curling the phone to her chest as she hopped with glee.

"What?" Gary asked from the archway, startling her.

"Nothing." She recovered quickly, returning to her preparations.

He leaned against the doorframe. "Ok. It's Christmas morning. You're not usually this chipper," he observed.

"Well, Christmas has gotten better over the years." She beamed at him, unwilling to reveal Ben's secret. "Are you getting that shower?"

"I bettered," he replied gruffly, still not convinced. "I'll try not to wake the kids."

"Ok. The girls will be here shortly, and we'll get everyone up then." Swooshing past him, she turned on the lamps so she could inspect his work while he bathed.

Going down the line, she grinned at the tiny tricycle that Lane would enjoy. Next to it, a bright pink two-wheeler sported training wheels, but it was the last one she really wanted a good look at.

"He'll be fine," Gary called quietly, then turned to the stairs to make his way up.

Her fingers on the bright chrome, Candy traced the line of the handlebars fondly. "I sure hope so," she mumbled to herself. They had debated the purchase long and hard, and in the end her mate had convinced her that Daks was old enough to learn to ride. Especially if they were going to make such a purchase for the younger two.

Turning to the dollhouse, she grinned broadly, as the term gave no indication of the massive neighborhood he had constructed. "It's perfect," she whispered, admiring the set of small buildings that her children would surely enjoy. "Woo-woos is their favorite game."

"Candy," a woman's voice called from the adjacent room.

"Coming, Mom." She sighed, ready to go help her mother prepare to face the day.

EIGHTEEN

Presents to Present

"OH, THIS IS ADORABLE!" Holly squealed as the Ford children setup their new town.

"Yes, I'm glad Santa brought them something besides bikes with all that snow on the ground. It'll be months before we can get outside and use them," Gary lamented from his cushioned chair.

"Fun for all year," Lanelle agreed in her gravelly tone.

Snapping a few pictures, Eve giggled. She and Roger had gifted vehicles to pair with their new village. "I'm glad the size is such a good match."

"It wouldn't have mattered," Roger countered. "They would have loved their new toys either way."

In the kitchen, Caroline, Holly and Candy were busy putting the final touches on their meal when a black sedan pulled around to park behind the house. Peeking out, Candy breathed, "Finally." She had been bursting with her news about Mel and Ben but had so far managed to keep it secret, keenly aware it would be his news to share. "Ben and Melody are here!" she called loudly. Opening the door, she let them in. "Wow, that's a good-sized pack. The kids have made quite a haul this year."

Grinning, Melody shook her head. "I'm afraid I have no gifts for them."

"Then what's in the sack?" Holly asked, admiring the size of her bundle.

"I bought a few gifts for the adults," Melody replied cryptically. "Come and sit, and I'll hand them out. Unless you want me to wait until after dinner."

"No, we may have another hour on this turkey," Carol lamented as she closed the oven. "It's not cooking as quickly as I had hoped."

"Good, then let's have some wine and chairs," Ben instructed, opening the fridge. "My Melody has presents to present."

"Well, if this is for the adults, we should shift the new woo-woos to the den," Eveline suggested.

"I'll do it," Gary moaned.

"I'll help," Ben volunteered, scooping up a box to fill it with their new cars.

Gathering the largest building, Gerald implemented with the move, placing the structures he had so carefully constructed in their new homes. "This has become more like the playroom rather than a den," he observed as his children settled in and resumed the game.

"It's wonderful," Ben agreed. Slapping his almost brother on the shoulder, he praised, "You're a lucky man."

Gary observed his jovial grin. "Thanks." Rubbing his chin, he added quietly, "Are you and my wife up to something?"

"No!" Benjamin appeared shocked. "Why? Did she say something?"

"No!" Gary laughed loudly. "But you both seem to be in a really good mood. And you know I love my wife, but she isn't usually so pleasant at Christmas time."

Ben's face burst into a full grin. "You'll find out soon enough," he teased.

Returning to the living room, Gary reclaimed his comfy chair and accepted his glass of wine. Across from him, Candy curled into her favorite end of the couch, while Ben took the opposite end, leaving the space between them for Melody. Bringing in chairs from the kitchen, everyone soon had a place to sit and a chilled libation to sip while their newest member shared her Christmas spirit.

Candy giggled merrily as her eyes darted around their circle. "I guess giving Christmas speeches has become a Ford family tradition!" She raised her crystal to toast her friend. "Does this mean you've accepted your place within our bubble?"

Ben chortled, shaking his head. "It's been a long, few months, hasn't it."

"Indeed, it has," Melody agreed, anxiously rocking between her toes and heels as she stood before them. "Months ago, I had no clue I would be standing here." She raised a hand to indicate Gary and Roger in turn. "I've come a long way in such a short time, and I only have all of you to thank."

Blinking rapidly to hide her tears, Mel turned to her parcel and opened the drawstring with trembling digits. Freed, she reached in and removed a few brightly colored boxes. Handing out each in turn, she presented the members with a gift and a heartfelt thank you.

"Roger, you trickster. You gave me exactly what I needed to feel safe in your company. Thank you." He accepted his gift with a firm nod.

"Gary, you were a wonderful driver, and I will never look at ice cream the same way again," she teased, offering a long, slender box.

The girls giggled when they were presented with a large

package to share. "To the many evening get-togethers to come," Melody hinted, giving the top a tap with her nails.

She didn't wait for replies and moved quickly through her list. Dropping hints as to what each parcel might contain, she noticed they waited patiently for all to be addressed before the unwrapping commenced. "You are all so polite!" she praised. "I thought people loved to tear into packages as soon as they were presented." Reaching the bottom of her sack, she sighed. "I have one more, and then you can open them, I guess."

The group laughed anxiously, each having enjoyed their moment of admiration, but Eve boldly challenged the younger woman. "Did you save me for last on purpose?"

"I'm afraid that I did," Melody confessed. "But I need for you to open yours. I need for you to see it before I say what I need to say."

"Oh my," Eve gasped, at a rare loss for words. Accepting a slender box, about two by eight inches, her hands held it tenderly as she guess the contents. "I love jewelry. How did you know?"

"I'm afraid this isn't any old ordinary bracelet." Melody breathed heavily, waiting while Eve's aged fingers opened the wrapping and pulled back the tissue.

"Oh my," Eve gasped once more. "It's beautiful." She lifted the bracelet filled with charms to examine it more closely.

"When I met you, I believed you were a crochety old woman," Mel explained. "But you quickly put me in my place, and I have followed your mantra ever since. For weeks, I have told myself that my condition was simple to fix. Mind over matter." She laughed nervously, dabbing at her eyes to prevent the deluge. "And although I'm not ready to join the world at large, for now at least, I do know that I'm in a better place."

Seeing his wife's inability to speak, Roger interjected, "Welcome to the bubble."

"Hear hear!" the group agreed, raising their glasses to toast their newest member.

"Thank you," Eve croaked, fondling the plethora of charms. Seeing a tiny firetruck, she caressed the shiny metal. "They represent us," she assumed.

"Yes. I found it quite cathartic to search for things that characterized the people I have grown so fond of these last few months," Melody explained. "At first, I thought it was for me. Something to symbolize each of you in my new life. But then I realized that the center of this circle is actually you. With your Eve advice."

"Amen," Candy whispered, recalling how Eve had come to her rescue so many years before. "You are the matriarch of our family, Eveline. The rock upon which we all lean."

"Does this mean you'll be coming around more often?" Gary asked cautiously. "I mean, it's hard to imagine you being cured completely in such a short time."

"Oh, I'm far from cured." Melody inhaled deeply, then sighed. "Last night, I realized I still have a long way to go. I only made it through the festival on sheer willpower and a strong arm to lean on."

"Thanks, love," Benjamin breathed.

"I never could have done that if you hadn't been there. And I never could have let you into my life if you hadn't spent a few years creeping your way in," she teased, giving the group a chuckle. "It's hard to believe, but deep down I know that it was the pandemic that saved me."

"So, you aren't going to hide back in your own little world?" Holly asked, her eyes glistening with misty joy.

"Oh, no. I'm moving forward," Melody announced. "I'm planning on spending a great deal of time here, if you will have me."

"You know we will," Lanelle pronounced loudly. "We welcome you to the bubble."

"Good," Mel clipped. "Then I look forward to more time and the healing to come. Especially since I'm going to be trimming my practice. I feel like I need to..." Her voice trailed away, and she appeared thoughtful. "I chose my career as a way to hide from my fears. I enjoy what I do, but I feel like I need to step back and explore new opportunities." Her gaze fixed on Ben, she smiled. "I have a whole life before me that wasn't there before, and you could say that I'm eager to explore it."

Meeting her stare, Benjamin simply raised his hand from its relaxed position on the back of the sofa, indicating for her to join him. Without hesitation, she crossed the room and sank onto the cushion to curl into the safety of his embrace.

Epilogue

CANDY WALKED CASUALLY through the manor across the street from her home, a yellow legal pad in her hand. "I think this room should be red." She drew a box on the sheet of paper and began a list. "We need a sofa, a twin bed, and all the trimmings."

"I think we should add a crib," Holly chimed in.

"Or a toddler bed," Carol suggested.

Candice's pencil scrawled the notes, her mind distracted to the last time she had undertaken such a task. "You know, we did this before we adopted Joy. Gary and I did. A whole list of things we had to do and fix." She chuckled at the recollection. "It was a real pain, but worth every minute of it."

"Well, we don't have the finances of the Fords, so it will take us a while to get things in order over here," Holly pointed out sullenly. "I figure we will get two bedrooms dressed out and start the upstairs lounge. The rest will come from money earned via the rents and donations we collect."

"I'm sure glad Melody is on board. It will be nice to offer free medical care to the girls," Carol soothed. "We'll get by."

Candy's phone vibrated in her pocket. Pulling it out, she

groused, "Oh, shoot. I forgot, I have to meet Cathy this afternoon. She's planning a celebration for my graduation." Flipping to the back of her notes, she stared at the map they had started with. "I think you're right. These are a lot of rooms, and we have to install the privacy door for you two and Gracie. Closing off that end of the hallway is a priority in my book."

She sighed, recalling how their plan had slowly come together. Although she found Glenda's offer tempting, the trio decided the time had come to convert Carol and Holly's mansion into a half-way house. When they were finished, they would have the five bedrooms that each held a private bath transformed into small, one-room apartments. Their room, and the adjacent one that Grace occupied, would be given the privacy door, so it could be locked, with no access to their guests. "Yes, that is a priority," she added, tapping that part of the drawing before moving to the rest.

One of the three remaining bedrooms would be converted into a community family room, and the other would become a second kitchen, leaving the third for a guest room or storage. "Our new adventure is going to be amazing. I can't wait to start filling these rooms, and our future, with the same love and grace that has been given to me."

"To all of us," Carol hummed in agreement.

"Four women for women," Holly quipped before leaving to attend to their daughter, who fussed in her crib in the other room.

Thank You

Thank you for reading, and I hope that you have enjoyed the 2022 installment of the Sweet Christmas Series. Look for a new adventure for Gary and Candy at Christmas next year. ~ Sam

Books in this series include:
Christmas Candy (2015)
Christmas Eve (2016)
Christmas Carol (2017)
Christmas Joy (2018)
Christmas Holly (2019)
Christmas Lane (2020)
Christmas Bell (2021)
Christmas Melody (2022)

About the Author

Anyone who knows me could tell you, I am a friendly kind of person, never met a stranger and take up conversations anywhere at any time. I work hard, and my mind never seems to shut down, as I wake up often in the middle of the night with ideas pouring out and demanding to be dealt with. Of course that means much of my books were written in the middle of the night.

I grew up and still live in the great state of Texas where everything is bigger, where we have warm weather and a central location. I love my state, my town, and my family, which includes my four sons, my significant other, and many friends as well.

I have thoroughly enjoyed writing this story and hope that you will love reading it just as much. And of course, there will be many more adventures to come.

You can follow Samantha Jacobey at:
Website: www.SamJacobey.com
Facebook: https://www.facebook.com/SamJacobey
Twitter: https://twitter.com/SamJacobey

Also by SAMANTHA JACOBEY

https://www.lavishpublishing.com/authors/samantha-jacobey/

A New Life Series – an epic adventure, TORI FARRELL's life IS one wild story... escaped from a biker gang and running from drug lords... used by the FBI and hoping to protect her present from her past... IT'S DARK - IT'S BRUTAL, and it's WORTH EVERY MINUTE OF IT!! (Mature read, 18+ for graphic sexual content and violence, including rape)

Summer Spirit Novella Series - no one EVER had a summer romance like this… Charlie visits another plane, parallel to our own, where Summer Angels and Dark Angels battle over the fate of man. A unique twist on an old idea that will keep you guessing; will Charlie and Clarisse ever find their HEA? (New adult)

Teach Me to Prey – in this standalone thriller, JASON TRUITT and his friends have gotten their way for years. Deceit, sex, and foul play aren't normally covered in the curriculum, but they're doing whatever it takes to get under BECKY STEWART's skin. When one of the boys turns up dead, it's a race against time to save the others; a STUNNING STORY that will get your heart racing and leave you breathless by the end… (New Adult)

The Binding (Unexpected Magic #1) - One cursed diary will change two strangers forever...Can Meri and Rider use her mother's old book to figure out why someone is after them? Or will the guilty party succeed, ripping the tome away before killing them and then slithering back into the darkness… (New Adult)

The Wicked Awakened (Unexpected Magic #2) – a Halloween novel; a five-hundred-year-old witch wants to turn SARAH MATTHEWS' body into her new home… A twisted tale involving a coven hell bent on seeing that she succeeds. Who will come out on top in this epic battle of wills? (Mature read, 18+ for graphic sexual content and violence)

The Irrevocable Series - From affluent beginnings, BAILEY DEWITT's life has become a broken mess... after her parents died unexpectedly, she didn't think it could get any worse. But when the arrogance of man catches up and puts the entire world into a dooms-day spiral, there will be only ONE PLACE she can run to - the ONE PLACE she wanted desperately to escape. (New Adult)

The Dragon of Eriden Series - Amicia Spicer led a simple life, until she discovered it had all been a lie… On her deathbed, Arely Spicer confessed to her only daughter that she had been found by, not born to her mother and father. Sad news to be certain, the idea of having a family of flesh and blood waiting to be reunited sent the young, independent woman on the adventure of a lifetime. Little did she know, a dragon's heart beat within her chest and her journey would be more perilous than she could have imagined... (New Adult)

Also from our Lavish family

Love on the Double Duo
By L.A. Remenicky
https://books2read.com/LoveDoubleDuo

The Monroe brothers fall fast, they fall hard, and they fall forever. But the road to true love isn't always easy.

Loving Jessie's Girl – Book 1: Until AJ Monroe left Indiana after college he had always lived in his identical twin brother's shadow. He had made a life for himself in Denver, Colorado, away from Jessie, away from Indiana. But when AJ feared for his brother's safety, he left everything behind to step back into the shadow he thought he had outgrown. Finding his brother was AJ's only concern...until he met Jessie's girl.

Fiercely independent, Rina Abbot hid her true situation from everyone, including her best friend, Jessie. Out of money and unable to care for her rescue dogs she had no choice but to accept the help of the handsome stranger with a familiar face.

Afraid to trust him, she tried to ignore the feelings he stirred within her as they searched for his missing brother.

But secrets never stay secrets for long.

Finally open about their feelings for each other, Rina's secrets began to wreak havoc on their lives. Would Rina's secrets force AJ to give up his dream of loving Jessie's girl?

Beyond Duty – Book 2: After serving in the Marine Corps, Jessie Monroe has finally found a life beyond war. He's focused on

being an EMT and helping his best friend rescue dogs, until he happens upon a curvy blonde stranded

with a flat tire and no jack.

On the run from her past, Dori Graham is slow to trust any man, and she tries to ignore the spark of

interest she feels for her handsome savior, but a friendship grows between them.

When Dori's past invades her new life, Jessie vows to rescue her. Saving her will take him beyond duty

and into his own personal hell. Calling upon his training as a Marine and the depth of his feelings for

Dori, Jessie will need the mental strength to battle to save her and, ultimately, save himself.

Between the Trees

Kathy Moczerniak

https://www.lavishpublishing.com/authors/kathy-moczerniak/

A beautiful coming of age with a dark side that one teenager must fight to overcome...

Beyond Kathryn Lucas' first memory of her father's tree lay a dysfunctional path of violence, heartbreak, and secrets within a family severely entrenched in the vicious cycle of abuse. A lifetime of fear drives her from her home, and the teenage girl finds refuge with an aunt and uncle determined to protect their niece.

Distressing flashbacks unravel in Kathryn's fragile mind among the turmoil encircling her as she struggles through adolescence and descends into her pain-ridden past. When the summation of her unsettling memories allows the darkness to overtake her, she becomes desperate to unearth the light.

Inspired by a true story, Kathryn must hold on tightly to those who love her, searching for her place in a world threatening to break her as she fights to overcome life's betrayals before she is deprived of her future.

The Hunter Series
Sara J. Bernhardt
https://books2read.com/HuntersTrilogySet

Jane Callahan is a reclusive, seventeen-year-old high school student dealing with the death of her beloved brother. Her home in Southern California with her mother is a constant reminder of her loss and pain. In hopes of escaping her past she moves to North Bend Oregon to live with her father, where she meets a beautiful boy named Aidan Summers.

Jane is intrigued by his looks as well as his unusual ways of attempting to get her attention. After months of uncommon conversation and frustration, an uncertain romance brews between Jane and Aidan, but Aidan has a ghastly secret that could destroy everything.